SWEET DREAMS

INDIGO BAY SWEET ROMANCE SERIES

Stacy Claflin

www.stacyclaflin.com

To receive 3 free novels from the author, sign up here.
stacyclaflin.com/newsletter

ONE

Sky Hampton pulled into the parking spot, double-checked the address on the quaint building, and turned off the car. The little Yorkie in the passenger seat gave a curious whine.

She stretched and rubbed Pixie's head. "Yeah, I'm ready to get out, too." Sky unbuckled the doggie seat belt and held open her large Coach bag for the pup to hop into. Once Pixie was settled, Sky got out of her Audi. The humidity clung to her like a wet towel. She slid on sunglasses, donned a hat, then headed for the building marked *Guest Services*.

"Are we going to be guests, or will we settle?" Sky pulled at her collar. "We're not in Oregon anymore, are we?"

Pixie gave a little yap. Her tail whipped lightly against the purse.

"You're right. That's exactly what we want. Something completely different. We'll adjust to this—assuming they have AC." It was only springtime, and the heat and humidity were already oppressive. She didn't even want to think about what the summer might be like. At least they could ease into the heat.

Sky pushed the door open and took in the little building. No one sat at the reception desk, and everything was quiet. A plate of sticky buns sat next to a pot of coffee.

"Hello?" Sky called.

A brunette about her age came out from around the corner. She smiled wide at Sky. "Hi! I didn't realize we had guests." She nodded toward Sky's purse. Pixie had popped her head out.

Sky rubbed the Yorkie's head. "I'm Sky Hampton. I'm renting a cottage."

"Oh, yes. I talked with you on the phone. My name's Zoe." She typed on the computer. "Have a bun or some coffee. Do you want to take off your sunglasses?"

Sky didn't reach for the refreshments or her sunglasses.

Zoe glanced up. "You should really try one. They're from Sweet Caroline's, and they're to die for."

"I'll keep that in mind, thanks." Sky smiled.

An awkward silence followed.

Zoe quickly grabbed a key and some paperwork. "You're in the dark blue cottage. Looks like you're paid for the month. Staying longer, by any chance?"

"Hopefully. We'll see."

"Vacationing?"

Sky chewed on her lower lip. What was the best way to describe her situation? She'd probably get asked about that a lot in the small town of Indigo Bay. "It's complicated." That would have to do for now.

"Hmm. Well, I hope you enjoy your stay. Let us know as soon as you know if you'll be staying or leaving."

"Sure thing."

Zoe shoved the papers across the desk. "Just sign where the X's are."

Sky grabbed a pen and signed.

"If you need anything, the numbers are on this sheet." Zoe handed it to her. "If you have anything that needs fixin', Jace is your man. He's the cottage handyman."

"Sounds good."

Zoe handed her some other papers and a key. "Hope you enjoy your time in the cottages. There's lots to do. The beach is real close, and so is a lot of other stuff. Stop by Sweet Caroline's for refreshments—it's a great place to meet people, too."

"Thanks so much." Sky returned the smile that hadn't left Zoe's face, and took her stuff.

"Don't forget, if you need anything, just holler."

"Will do." Sky tucked the papers in her purse next to Pixie and headed back to the car. It was a short drive to the dark blue cottage. She parked in front and studied the structure. It was bigger than she'd imagined and looked well cared for. She scratched Pixie behind the ear. "Ready to see our new home?"

Pixie licked her hand.

Sky got out of the car and set the pup on a patch of grass, holding tightly to the leash. Pixie jumped around and sniffed the ground. She marked her territory and then went right back to sniffing, her tail and ears both high in the air. She barked and panted, giving her seal of approval.

A couple walking down the street waved and called hello.

Sky returned the wave and hurried to the cottage, eager to settle in. As soon as she opened the door, a wave of cool air greeted them. Sky smiled and let go of the leash. Pixie ran inside, her claws tapping on the hardwoods as she explored. Sky stepped in, closed the door behind her, and took in the sight of her new home.

Most everything was in dark hardwoods, and she loved it. The fully furnished cottage made her feel like kicking her feet up and relaxing after the long drive. She set her purse on the kitchen table and headed back out to the Audi, making half a dozen trips before remote-locking the sedan and locking herself inside the little bungalow.

"Pixie! Where are you?"

Tapping sounded before the little copper-and-black fluff-ball appeared around a corner.

"How do you like it?"

Pixie ran around her legs until Sky scooped her up and snuggled her. "Feel free to wear yourself out running around. We don't have to get back in the car anytime soon."

The pup covered her in kisses until she couldn't take it, and Sky set her down. Pixie scampered off, sliding around a corner. Sky chuckled and then looked at her pile of bags and luggage. As tempting as it was to crash on the overstuffed couch and close her eyes, she really just wanted to get settled in. It had been a long drive from Oregon, and she'd barely slept so she could make the best time possible.

Her body ached, but she reached for a few of the bags needed in the bedroom and searched her new home until she found it on the other side of the cottage. An hour later, she was fully unpacked and ready for a nap.

Pixie skittered into the bedroom. She yapped and jumped around.

"Aren't you ready for a nap?"

"Ruff!"

Sky rubbed her eyes. "Right. You slept the whole way here."

Pixie tugged on Sky's pants—she'd put them on that morning in Kearney, Nebraska out of habit from the chilly weather she was used to in Oregon. The pup continued pulling.

Sky picked her up. "You're lucky you're so cute, but

we still need to break you of that habit."

Pixie squirmed until Sky set her down and followed her to the sliding glass door. On the other side, a family of ducks wandered around, quacking.

"Oh," Sky gushed. "They're so cute."

Pixie barked.

"Hush. You'll scare them away." She picked her up and rubbed between Pixie's ears.

A loud beep sounded from somewhere, followed by a *thunk, thunk.*

The pup raised her ears and looked at Sky.

Thunk. Thud. Crash!

Silence echoed around them.

The AC had died.

TWO

Jace Fisher dug through his toolbox, grumbling about the AC at the dark blue cottage. He needed to convince Dallas it was time to replace the unit. Jace could only do so much for a machine on its last legs, and with a new resident calling on her first day, it just looked bad for the whole resort.

He stuck the tools he needed into his smaller box and headed outside. Jace lowered his baseball cap in hopes of avoiding eye contact with everyone he came across—though most of the regulars knew he preferred to keep to himself and usually respected that.

When he came to the dark blue cottage, he set the toolbox down and knocked. "Here to fix the AC!"

The door opened, and in front of him stood a tall, slender brunette with enchanting deep brown eyes. Their gazes locked, and Jace studied her. She seemed familiar, like he knew her, but he was certain he'd never met her before. He'd have remembered those eyes. Of that much he was sure.

He cleared his throat and stuck out his hand. "Jace Fisher. I'm here to fix your AC unit."

She shook his hand. Hers was so smooth and soft, and it smelled fruity and sweet. He quickly pulled his hand away.

"Thank you." A tiny, fluffy dog ran to her feet and she scooped it up. "I don't know what happened," she said quickly. "It made all these noises, and then just went out. Oh, I'm Sky Hampton."

Hampton. Why did that seem familiar? "Nice to meet you, Sky."

She stepped back and pulled her long hair away from her neck and fanned herself, balancing the fur ball. "Come on in. It's over here."

Jace gave a nod and picked up his toolbox. "I'm familiar with the cottages."

"Oh, of course. Well, I'll just stay out of your way, then."

"I'll do my best to be out of your hair as soon as possible." He hurried over to the living room and got to work. It was the same problem it'd been for the last few months. He fixed it quickly, having done the same thing numerous times before.

It roared to life, blowing out cool air. Not cold, but cool. He scratched his chin and tinkered with it some more, not getting any colder air. Jace checked the coolant level. That wasn't the problem.

"Miss," he called.

She appeared, the dog following at her heels. "You can call me Sky."

Jace nodded. "I just want to show you something."

Sky came over. "What's that?"

"See this knob?" He tapped the temperature control. She nodded.

"If this thing goes out, hit about a foot above it. Sometimes that'll kick it into shape. If not, give me another call. In the meantime, I'm calling Dallas, the owner of the cottages, to request we replace the entire unit. I apologize that you have to deal with it—it should've already been taken care of."

Sky smiled sweetly. "It's fine. Thanks so much for fixing it."

He shrugged. "Not a problem. It's my job."

"Hey, do you want a water or something? I don't have much else to offer. I still need to go shopping."

"I'm fine. Hope you enjoy your stay."

"Thanks." She walked him to the door and waved as he left.

Jace gave a quick wave and headed back to his place. Once there, he replaced his tools into the larger box and headed inside to finish his supper. After eating, he gave Dallas a call. It went to voicemail.

"Dallas, this is Jace. We need a new AC unit in the dark blue cottage ASAP. As soon as our newest guest arrived, it went out again. If you need me to pick one up, just say the word." He ended the call and walked over to the sliding glass door. It was another nice night—as most were in Indigo Bay.

He grabbed his sketch book and pencils and headed outside to his favorite little hiding spot, nestled in between some trees. A root stuck up out of the ground at the perfect angle to be a seat. It was just far enough away from the main part of the beach that nobody ever bothered him there.

Jace made himself comfortable and found an empty page in his book. He glanced around, deciding what to draw this evening. In the distance, a whooping crane stuck its beak into the water and spread its wings. Jace pulled out a red pencil, starting with the bright spot on the bird's head. He drew quickly, and carved the image into his mind knowing it wouldn't be long before a beach ball or a couple walking hand-in-hand would scare the creature away.

He wasn't sure how much time had passed when the masterpiece was finally complete. Jace studied the drawing of the crane fishing for something in the slightly wavy water. He added some more red to the top of its head and then leaned back against the tree, marveling that the bird was still in the same spot, poking around.

It flung its head back, splashing water. A crab squirmed around in its beak.

"Look at that." A rare smile spread across Jace's face. Would the bird actually eat the clawed sea creature?

A toddler ran toward the bird, screaming at the top of his lungs. The crane spread out its wide wings, blocking Jace's view of the crab, and flew away.

So much for that. He returned the red pencil to the pouch and watched as the boy's mother chased after him, carrying a baby.

Jace's blood ran cold.

Was that Alisha? He leaned forward and squinted, his supper threatening to make a reappearance. It *was* Alisha. Ben ran over, catching up with them.

What were they doing back in town? Visiting family? Or showing up to rub their happiness in Jace's face?

Jace folded his arms and glowered at the woman who'd left him at the altar, taking his best man and lifelong friend with her. The hurt sliced through his heart with as much pain as it had the day of his wedding, when neither the bride nor best man had ever showed.

THREE

Sky finished off the protein bar and threw the wrapper in the garbage. "That wasn't the best dinner I've ever had." She glanced at Pixie. "You ate better than I did tonight. Tomorrow we'll find a grocery store."

The pup yapped and then ran around in circles.

She laughed. "Probably should get you outside for some exercise." Sky stretched and rose, hoping the air had cooled. It was darker outside, giving her hope.

The way the evening light shone in through the windows made the cottage seem almost magical.

"Look at this lighting. I've got to get some pictures for my blog. This place is adorable in the daytime, but now—it's fantastic."

Pixie jumped around, obviously not caring one bit about the lighting.

Sky pulled out her phone and snapped about fifty pictures from just about every angle, capturing the Yorkie as much as she could. Her readers followed her for the fashion advice, but they stayed because of Pixie—the real star of the blog.

She backed up the pictures to the cloud before grabbing the leash.

The AC unit made a sputtering noise. Sky groaned, but then remembered Jace's advice. She went over to the unit and hit it with the side of her fist about a foot above the knob. It clunked a couple times, and then returned to the normal sounds.

"I hope they replace this soon."

It made a clacking noise, as if to say it hoped they *didn't* replace it.

She whacked it one more time, and it went back to normal without complaint. Pixie jumped around her feet. Sky latched the leash to her collar and they headed out back. It took forever to actually make it to the beach with the little dog stopping every two feet to sniff around and occasionally mark her territory.

The sun was starting to set, and the sky had gorgeous shades of purple and pink intermixed with some orange. The water reflected the colors, taking her breath away. She pulled out her phone and snapped a ton of pictures. Her next blog post would be *amazing*. The readers were going to go nuts over her new home.

Sky laughed and had fun as she chased Pixie dancing through the sand. The best part was that though they passed people, nobody paid her any attention. It was still too early to tell for sure, but so far, Indigo Bay seemed like the right place to be. Of all the people she'd passed and met, not one had mistaken her for Aspen. Nobody had run up to her, begging for an autograph or selfie with her.

She could finally breathe.

They stayed on the beach until Pixie tired. Sky scooped her up, dusted the sand off her fur, and headed back to the cottage, yawning and hungry. As soon as they stepped inside, Pixie ran to her little bed and fell asleep.

"Wish I could do the same. I won't be able to sleep until I eat something more than that protein bar." She pulled her long hair into a low ponytail, put on a pink plaid bucket hat and big sunglasses—just in case. She'd been okay so far, but she wasn't taking any chances.

After double-checking on Pixie, she grabbed her purse and headed outside. She just wanted something quick. Zoe had said Sweet Caroline's would fit the bill for that, and it was close. Sky held the map under the porch light then headed for the coffee shop and found it easily.

Inside, the atmosphere was warm. People were sprawled across the cafe, some sitting on couches and others at tables. Sky kept her sunglasses on as she strolled over to the counter and smiled at the pretty brunette who was about her mom's age.

The lady smiled. "Welcome to Sweet Caroline's. I'm Caroline."

Sky extended her hand. "I'm Sky Hampton."

Caroline shook her hand. "Welcome to Indigo Bay. Feel free to take off your glasses and make yourself comfortable. I like folks to think of this as their second home."

"I'm fine for now, but thanks." Sky had gotten used to wearing sunglasses inside—not that it always kept people from thinking she was Aspen. She could wear army fatigues, complete with black all over her face, and some of Aspen's super-fans would still mistake Sky for her sister.

"Well, bless your heart." Caroline tucked some of her short hair behind her ear and studied Sky. "Want some coffee? Something to eat?"

Coffee sounded way too strong. She wanted to go to sleep soon. "Maybe something to eat." She glanced at the sandwiches behind the counter and pointed to an overstuffed one called the Oceanic. "I'll try that one."

Caroline reached for it. "What'cha want to drink? This sandwich has a little kick to it."

"Maybe a Coke." That would have just enough caffeine to keep her going until crashing. She yawned just thinking about the fluffy bed in the cottage.

"What kind?" Caroline asked.

Sky met her gaze. "Of what?"

"You said you wanted a coke."

"Right."

"Oh," Caroline said. "You must be from up north.

We call all the soft drinks a coke around here, sweetie. You want a Coca-Cola brand coke?"

"Or water. Water's fine."

"Don't worry about it." She grabbed a glass bottle of Coke and rang up the bill.

Sky handed her a card and then hurried over to an open table, eager to eat in peace. She dug into the sandwich filled with shrimp, sprouts, avocado, and something a little spicy. It was really good, and she scarfed it down, only then realizing just how hungry she'd let herself get.

Caroline walked around the coffee shop with a rag, spot-cleaning various surfaces. She came over to Sky and wiped a spot at the other end of the table. "How is it?"

"Delicious." Sky wiped the corner of her mouth with a napkin. "I could eat that every day."

"Feel free. We make those daily—they're a staple. Mind if I have a seat?"

"Sure. I'm not much of a conversationalist right now, though."

Caroline raked her fingers through her hair. "Just get in today?"

Sky sipped her pop and nodded. "Drove from Oregon."

"Oh, my. That's a long ways. What brings you to Indigo Bay?"

"A friend vacationed here and thought I might like it."

Caroline arched a brow. "For a vacation?"

Sky shrugged. "We'll see."

"Looking for a quieter pace of life?"

"Something like that."

Caroline leaned back and tapped the table. "Well, I hope you like it here—and that you eventually feel comfortable enough to take off the sunglasses."

Sky could feel the request between the lines. She took a deep breath and removed the shades, sliding them into her purse.

"You're so pretty," Caroline said. "Why hide?"

A few tables away, a group of three teenage girls whispered to each other.

Sky sighed. *And it starts.* She turned back to Caroline. "I look a lot like a celebrity."

Caroline tilted her head. "I don't see it. Who?"

"Aspen Hampton."

"Hampton? Didn't you say your last name was Hampton?"

"That would be why I'm mistaken for her—all the time." From the corner of her eyes, Sky could still see the teens whispering. One pointed her way. Another slid her finger around a cell phone screen, probably comparing her with pictures of Aspen. It didn't matter that Aspen always had some crazy hair color—turquoise, magenta, violet, or anything unusual and attention-grabbing—and Sky always kept hers natural, she and Aspen had the same face. There was no getting around it.

"Sky?" Caroline's voice broke through her thoughts.

"Sorry." Sky turned to her and shook her head. "Like I said, I'm not—"

"No worries, dear. I'll be sure to let folks know to leave you alone."

She was overcome with gratitude. "You will?"

"Of course. If you ever need anything, just let me know. I know this town like the back of my hand."

The three girls came over to the table, whispering to each other.

Caroline waved them away. "Off with y'all. I know your mamas taught you better manners than this."

They scampered off, giggling and looking back at Sky.

"Thanks," Sky said.

Caroline rose and started to walk away. "Happy to help. I'd better get this place cleaned up."

Hope rose in Sky as she finished her drink. She felt like she'd actually made a friend.

FOUR

Jace stepped outside and breathed in the fresh morning air. For the moment, nothing needed to be fixed at the cottages, so he was going to take advantage of the quiet early hours and get some groceries. He adjusted the bill of his Panthers cap just above his eyes and hopped into his pickup.

Lucky for him, the parking lot was nearly empty. He could get in and out without having to talk to anyone. Jace parked near the front and went inside, taking his usual path around the store, sliding easy-to-make food into the shopping buggy.

He stopped at the pastry counter, trying to decide what to eat for breakfast. As usual, everything made his mouth water.

"Well, if it isn't Jace Fisher," came a familiar feminine voice from behind.

He spun around to see the blonde, seventy-ish southern belle. Lucille Sanderson wore a knee-length polka-dotted dress, high heels, and too much makeup.

She fluffed her perfectly styled hair and smiled.

"Hello, Miss Lucille," Jace muttered.

"What brings you in so early?"

"Gotta eat." He turned back to the pastries.

"What have you been up to?" Lucille stepped up to the counter, her shoes clacking on the floor with each step.

Jace took a deep breath. "Just taking care of the cottages." He turned to the kid behind the counter and pointed to some Danishes. "I'll take three of those."

"Sure thing." The kid gathered them into a box.

"How's your mama?" Lucille stared at Jace. "Doing okay?"

Jace didn't want to talk about her. "She's all right."

"Do you visit her much?" She pointed to some chocolate pastries. "I'll have an éclair."

"Several times a week." Jace took the box of pastries and set it in the buggy. He took off, hoping to lose her, but he didn't even make it to the next aisle before he heard her shoes hurrying his way.

"How does Claire like the Manor?"

He turned to Lucille. "She likes the assisted living home just fine, ma'am. I don't mean to be rude, but I need to get going."

"Does the poor dear remember you?"

"Sometimes. Why don't you stop by and visit her? I'm sure she'd love your company."

"Maybe I will. Does she get many guests?"

"Not really. Excuse me. I have to—"

"And what about you?" Lucille stepped close enough that he could smell her heavy floral perfume. "I never see you around. Are you seeing anyone?"

Jace choked on air. "No, and I'm not lookin', either."

Lucille pulled out a small mirror and looked at it. "I ask because my daughter's niece is coming to town, visiting family. Maggie's a real sweet girl. Why, I'll bet she could pull you right out of your shell. You used to be such an outgoing boy before your brother's—"

"Sorry to be rude, but I really have to go. Have a nice day." Jace hurried away, fast enough that he was sure she couldn't catch up to him in those towering heels. He raced to the checkout line even though he needed a few more things—he could live without them.

Jace glanced over his shoulder as he exited the building. Lucille was paying for her pastry. He practically threw his bags into the passenger seat, barely took the time to shove the buggy to the return area, and then squealed the tires on the way out. He breathed a sigh of relief.

Now all he'd have to do was keep avoiding her, and that might be easier said than done in a place like Indigo Bay.

He made it home quickly and put his groceries away as he checked for messages, but everything seemed to be running just fine in the cottages. Dallas still hadn't called about that AC unit in the dark blue cottage. Jace might just have to go over to his office and talk to his boss face to face.

He grabbed one of the Danishes and sat at the table. His mind wandered back to seeing Alisha and Ben at the beach with their two kids. His stomach knotted just thinking about it—not that he still had any feelings left for Alisha. He was just glad that he found out about their relationship before getting married, even if he had been standing at the altar like some fool wondering what was going on.

Jace could still hear the whispers running through the crowd and the pitiful expressions—that was the worst part. He didn't want pity from anyone. Not even after being humiliated in front of everyone he cared about. Jace Fisher was a guy who didn't need anybody, and he'd spent the last few years proving that.

He took the next pastry, and as he ate, his mind wandered back to his conversation with Lucille. Not the part about her trying to set him up with her niece, but about his mom. It had been close to a week since he'd stopped by the Manor to visit her. Not that she was counting the days. It was rare when she even recognized him, and usually if she did, she mistook him for one of her brothers.

Jace left another message for Dallas about the AC unit and then he called the Manor to let them know he would be on his way over around lunchtime.

FIVE

Wet doggie kisses woke Sky. She rolled over, hoping to get more sleep. Pixie jumped over her and continued licking her face.

"Go back to sleep." She pulled the blanket over her head, but little paws stepped all over her, making it clear that Pixie wouldn't relent until Sky got out of bed. "When we get something permanent, it's going to have a fenced-in yard and a dog door."

The pup worked her way under the covers and licked Sky's arm.

"I'm awake, I'm awake." Rubbing her eyes, Sky sat up. "Let's get you outside."

Pixie panted happily. Sky rubbed the top of Pixie's head and tried to shake the sleepiness. The sun shone brightly from behind the curtains, splashing light onto the wall. Maybe it was later than it felt.

She yawned. "Okay, let's go outside." After pulling her hair into a messy bun, she slipped on a hoodie and flip-flops, and found Pixie's leash. As soon as she opened the sliding glass door, the warm, humid morning greeted her.

How did people live like this? She'd have to figure it out. Once outside, she started to adjust. Pixie took care of her business pretty quickly, so they were able to head back into the cool cottage. Yawning, Sky poured dog food into the bowl, and then she ate a protein bar for breakfast.

"We're going shopping after I get dressed."

Pixie yapped in reply.

"Glad you agree." Sky chuckled and headed back into the bedroom. She checked her phone. Everything had exploded with alerts—social media, texts, and new podcasts. That reminded her that she needed to update her blog as soon as possible.

She checked all of her notifications and then an hour later, climbed into the shower feeling more awake. Once she was done, she was more in the mood to work on her blog than to get groceries.

Sky pulled out her phone, turned on the video camera, and aimed it at her. "Hey, everybody! I've finally made it to my new home. Indigo Bay is totally as cute as I thought it'd be. You guys are going to love the videos and pictures. I'm inspired to do a beach-themed series— beachwear, a makeup or beach wave hairstyle tutorial, and more. Leave comments and let me know what *you* want! You've got to see this adorable cottage I'm staying in." She turned the phone out and scanned the bedroom and then took her fans on the grand tour.

By the time she had the video edited, she was hungry. That was what she got for barely having any breakfast. She uploaded the video to YouTube so her fans would have that much. She would work on the blog post after eating. Likes and comments came in before she had a chance to step away from her laptop.

Sky smiled and grabbed one of her large purses, figuring Pixie wouldn't be allowed to walk through the store on her leash. She called for the pup, and they headed out. Sky groaned as she locked the front door. It had gotten significantly warmer. She almost missed the crisp northwestern springtime weather. Pixie pranced toward the street, pulling on the leash.

She'd forgotten to look at the town map and tried to go by memory. People passed, waving friendly hellos. Not one person asked for an autograph or selfie with her. Sky found herself relaxing. Maybe this really would be a good place to settle down—assuming she could get used to the humidity. Sweat was already threatening to form—nobody else seemed as miserable as she was. Maybe she could acclimate, too.

Pixie stopped in front of a building that had a dog bowl filled with water and drank.

"That's thoughtful." Sky studied the black-paneled building. Happy Paws Pet Shop. It had two big picture windows, filled with pet items. "Oh, my gosh. That has to be the cutest thing I've ever seen. We have to go inside!"

She waited for Pixie to finish drinking—she'd emptied the bowl. Sky would have to go in and let the workers know, anyway. They went inside, Pixie prancing on in ahead of her. The door dinged above them.

"Greetings!" called a tall guy with sandy-brown hair. He looked to be about Sky's age. He shoved a large dog bed onto a shelf and walked over, extending his hand. "Welcome to the Happy Paws Pet Shop. I'm Sterling Montgomery, and my wife Violet is around here somewhere."

Sky shook his hand. "I'm Sky Hampton. Oh, and before I forget, we emptied your water bowl out there."

"Ah, thanks. I'll get to that. Is there anything I can help you find first?"

"We're just looking around for now. This place is so cute."

"That'd be Violet's doing. She has a real eye for that stuff. Are you vacationing?"

"Actually, I'm trying to figure out if this is where I want to move."

"Oh, really? Well, Indigo Bay is a wonderful place to live. But then again, I'm biased. Lived here my whole life."

Sky smiled. "Sounds like you know what you're talking about, then."

"I like to think so. Just don't tell Violet." He winked.

"Is someone here?" came a feminine voice. A pretty lady with long black hair came out from a doorway.

"We've got a customer. Sky Hampton is thinking of moving to Indigo Bay."

Violet's eyes widened. "You are?" She rushed over and grasped Sky's hands in hers. "You'll love it here. This is the best place you could pick." She glanced down at Pixie. "And who is this?"

"Pixie."

"What an adorable name!" Violet squatted and rubbed the pup's belly, speaking to Pixie in a high-pitched voice.

"So, can I help you find anything?" Sterling asked. "Otherwise, I should get back to stocking the beds."

"Actually, I don't suppose you know anyone looking for doggie play dates?" Sky asked.

Sterling shook his head. "Nope. Never had that request."

Violet sprang to her feet. "But what a great idea. Maybe that's a service we should offer."

"Let me know if you do. I'm going to look around if you don't mind."

"Of course," Violet said. "Just let us know if you need anything."

Sky stepped around a rack of leashes to look at the wall of dog toys. They had everything from doggie plushies to plastic squeakers to balls of every shape, size, and color.

STACY CLAFLIN

Sterling came over. "You mentioned a doggie play date?"

She nodded and grabbed a tiny plastic boomerang.

"I just had a thought. I don't know if you're interested, but I know someone who'd love a visit from your little Yorkie."

"Oh?" Sky raised an eyebrow.

He nodded. "My grandpa lives in the Manor—it's an assisted living home over by the boardwalk. He doesn't get a lot of guests, but he adores dogs. He's actually the one who instilled the love of pets in me from a young age."

"That actually sounds like fun." Sky put the boomerang back. "It's okay to just show up with a dog?"

"Oh, sure. The staff encourages anyone to stop by and visit. So many residents are lonely."

"Aw, that's sad. Yeah, Pixie and I would love to visit your grandpa. We'll head over today."

Sterling's face lit up. "Great. I'll call Nurse Gabby and let her know to expect you."

SIX

J ace walked up to the refurbished sprawling mansion and removed his cap when he reached the glass door. Inside, Gabby, one of the nurses, waved. The door buzzed as it unlocked, and Jace let himself in.

"How're ya doing, Jace?" Gabby smiled.

"Fine. You?"

"Not bad. Your mama's having a good day today. She was telling me all about her wedding day—showin' me pictures and everything."

"That's good news." He replaced and tipped his hat, then meandered down the hallway. Would his mom remember him? It had been so long since she'd been that lucid.

He came to her door and rapped several times.

"Come in!"

The door stuck as Jace pushed it open. He stepped inside, hoping—against his better judgment—that she'd recognize him.

"Bill." Her eyes lit up behind her thick glasses.

His heart sank. She thought he was her brother again. Jace forced a smile. "So good to see you, Claire."

She picked up an old photo album. "I was just thinking about my wedding day. I found the loveliest picture of you and Molly."

"Oh? Let me see." Jace walked over as she flipped through the pages.

"Here it is." She held it out, tapping a black and white photo. Sure enough, it was a picture of Uncle Bill and Aunt Molly.

Jace could see the family resemblance, but had a hard time understanding how his mom could mistake him for Bill—especially when she was looking back and forth between the image and him.

"Do you remember that day?" His mom beamed. "Albert was never more handsome than he was when we married."

"It was one of the best weddings I've seen." Jace helped her onto the rocking chair and then sat across from her. "You were the most beautiful bride."

"After Molly, of course." Mom smiled at him.

"Of course." Jace patted her hand. "What have you been doing lately? Anything fun?"

She looked deep in thought for a moment. "I don't know. You know, when Albert and I cut the cake, he wanted to smash it in each other's faces but I wanted to feed it to each other nicely. He teased me and said he was going to smash it anyway. But do you remember?

He was nice."

Jace nodded. "He was thoughtful like that."

"Was?" She stared at him.

"Is. Albert *is* thoughtful like that."

Her expression relaxed. "He's at work. No wife could ask for a better provider. You remember all those years we couldn't have kids? He lavished me with love and gifts, always letting me know he would adore me forever even if our family was only ever the two of us."

"He's a good man." Jace's voice cracked. It felt like he'd lost both of his parents, despite the fact that his mom sat in front of him.

"The boys are napping." She glanced at the clock on the wall. "They'll wake soon, if you want to stick around and say hi."

"I'd like that. Do you need anything? Some water?"

"Not now. I made some sweet tea earlier. I'll pour myself some later, once the icebox chills it."

Jace nodded. "You do love your sweet tea."

They sat in a comfortable silence as she flipped through the wedding album. After a while, she glanced back up at Jace. "Did I tell you what Connor did the other day?"

"No. Tell me."

She rambled on about something Jace's brother had done in kindergarten, but he couldn't concentrate on her words. He almost envied her memory loss. She had no idea that Dad and Connor were both long gone, but

Jace had to live with the loss of both. Kidney failure had killed his dad, and not long after that, a construction accident at work had taken Connor. Jace was pretty sure the shock of it all had shoved his mom into Alzheimer's. Before then, she'd been sharp as a tack, teaching art classes to the locals.

Finally, Jace couldn't take any more. He rose and stretched. "How about we go for a walk? You can introduce me to some of your neighbors."

"That sounds lovely. Let me powder my nose first."

"Sure thing." He picked up the album, flipping to the first page while she went into her bathroom. Jace smiled at the pictures of his parents so young and happy. They'd been just as happy when he was growing up, but they'd been a full twenty years older than in these old photos when he was born. It was hard not to wonder what it would've been like to know them then and get more time with them.

The bathroom door opened, and his mom stepped out wearing makeup like she used to.

"You look beautiful."

"Thank you, Bill. Where are we going, again?"

Jace rose and set the album down. "Just for a walk so you can introduce me to your neighbors."

She smiled and looped her arm through his. "Let's go."

They walked down the bright hall full of mostly closed doors. A few of the other residents waved from open doors.

"Who are they?" Jace hoped that seeing her current friends would help her memory.

"That there is Alice McGerty. Her husband must be out."

"I see." The McGertys had been their neighbors years earlier when Jace and Connor had been in elementary school. "Tell me about your other friends."

"Bob and Fiona Allens are good friends, but they're on vacation. They're taking a big cruise ship somewhere fancy."

"That sounds nice." The Allens had moved away when Jace had been a freshman in high school. He and his mom wandered around the Manor, not finding anyone who his mom actually remembered for who they were. But he wasn't going to give up. She'd finally tapped into some real memories—there was no reason to think she couldn't find the other ones, too.

SEVEN

Sky waved to Mark Montgomery. "It was wonderful to visit with you."

Sterling's grandfather smiled. "You and that little dog are welcome anytime. Come back whenever you want."

"I might just do that." She stepped out of his room and closed the door behind her. Pixie jumped around and sniffed the carpet. "You probably loved all that attention."

Her tail wagged back and forth as they walked down the hallway. There weren't many people walking the halls, but they all smiled at Sky and admired Pixie, some wanting to lavish more attention on the pup. Her heart warmed, and she wanted to return to the Manor regularly.

Sky gave a double-take as they passed a guy about her age in a Panthers hat, turning to enter a room with an elderly lady in thick glasses. Was that the handyman?

"Jace?"

He turned around. His eyes widened in matching surprise. "Sky, is it?"

She nodded. "We—"

A loud wailing noise sounded and red lights flashed from above.

Nurse Gabby ran down the hall to them. "It's a lock down! Get inside a room and lock the door!"

Sky looked around. "What's going on? Are we in danger?"

"Just get in a room!" Nurse Gabby ran off, telling others to get out of the hall.

"Come in here!" Jace stepped into a room and waved her over.

She picked up Pixie and ran inside.

Jace slammed the door shut and locked it. Then he pushed a shelf in front of it. "Can't be too safe."

"What's going on, Bill?" The elderly woman clung to Jace.

Sky's ears rang from the wailing, but at least it wasn't as loud in the room.

Jace helped the white-haired woman to sit on a rocking chair. "Some kind of excitement out there. We're safe in here. I promise."

The woman nodded and then studied Sky. "I know you. You're Frank and Mildred's daughter. What was your name again?"

Sky held out her hand. "I'm—"

"Elise! You're Elise."

"Actually, my name—"

Jace shook his head and mouthed, "Alzheimer's."

That explained her calling him Bill. Sky smiled and took the woman's hand. "I can't believe you remembered. Would you mind refreshing my memory? What's your name again?"

Jace threw her an appreciative glance.

"I'm Claire, and this is my brother Bill. I don't think you two ever met."

Sky smiled at Jace. "I think I met him once before. He was very helpful."

"That sounds like Bill." She rose from the chair. "If you'll excuse me, I need to powder my nose."

"Do you need help with anything?" Sky asked.

Claire shook her head. "Just make yourself comfortable. I have some tea if you'd like. Bill can show you where it is. I need to do something about the awful noise." She went into the bathroom and closed the door behind her.

"Thank you for going along with that," Jace said.

"No problem. Your grandma seems like a sweetheart."

He grimaced. "She's actually my mom."

"Oh, I'm sorry. I just assumed—"

"It's a common mistake." He stepped around the shelf and pressed his ear to the door. "I wonder what's going on out there."

"You can't hear anything?"

"Not over the alarm blaring."

Silence settled between them. Pixie squirmed in Sky's arms. She put her down, but kept a tight hold on the leash in case Claire was nervous around dogs.

Jace turned to her. "Do you know someone here in the Manor?"

"I came to visit a resident that I heard loves pets. I think Pixie made his whole month."

He smiled, and he was even more gorgeous. He had kind eyes, but they seemed to hold a lot of pain. "That's really nice of you. A lot of people with relatives in the Manor don't make it here all that often."

"It's fun to chat with the residents. They're all so happy to have someone to listen."

"True." He motioned toward the empty chairs. "May as well make yourself comfortable. We might be here a while."

Sky sat in a plush wheeled chair. Pixie jumped and Sky pulled her onto her lap. Jace sat near the door in a hard plastic seat.

"It must be hard to see your mom like that," Sky said. "I can't even imagine."

He frowned, a dark sadness washing over his face. "It just comes with the territory of having older parents."

It seemed like more than that, but Sky didn't know what to say. She got the feeling he didn't want to talk about it.

The bathroom door opened, and Claire sat back in the rocking chair. "What's your dog's name, Elise?"

"This is Pixie. Do you want to pet her?"

Claire's eyes lit up. "I'd love to."

Sky rose with Pixie and brought her over.

"What a lovely dog. She reminds me of Sophie. My best friend growing up—her name was also Claire—had a little dog like this, only without the fancy hair bows. Can I hold her?"

"Sure." Sky sat Pixie in Claire's lap. The pup sat and licked the old woman's hand.

Claire laughed with delight and patted Pixie. "You've always been such a good girl, Sophie."

Pixie continued licking.

Sky returned to her chair and watched the two interact.

"Thanks," Jace said. He removed his hat and ran his fingers through his hair, watching his mother with Pixie. Then he ran his fingers over his short-trimmed beard.

Sky's breath caught. Jace was tall, dark, handsome, and mysterious—a perfect combination that left her wanting to know more. It was so refreshing to be around a guy who didn't talk her ear off, and even better yet, he hadn't made one mention of Aspen in either interaction they'd had. And wow, was he good-looking.

He glanced at her.

She'd been caught staring. She recovered quickly. "Thanks for the tip about the AC. Every time I hit it above that knob, it starts working again."

"I'm gonna talk with Dallas about replacing that as soon as we're allowed to leave."

"It's no bother. I don't mind as long as hitting it keeps working."

Jace shook his head. "You shouldn't have to deal with that."

"Elise, can you help me with something?" Claire asked.

Sky jumped to her feet. "Sure thing."

"That alarm is giving me a headache. Can you find my aspirin? I can't remember where I left it."

"Sure. Let me check the bottles on your dresser. Hopefully, the noise will stop soon."

EIGHT

Jace watched in awe as Sky took care of his mom. She was such a natural, even more at ease with her than Jace, who had known her his entire life. She spoke easily, going along with the fantasy of being named Elise. If he didn't know better, he'd have thought they were the ones who'd known each other for thirty years and Jace had just met his mom. He couldn't recall ever being that relaxed around someone he'd just met.

His mom had always gotten along with the nurses and other Manor staff, but she really took to Sky—not that he could blame her. Sky treated his mom like the most important person in the world.

Sky was also beautiful. Her smile lit up the entire room.

Jace shook his head. He couldn't think like that. Focusing on how attractive Sky was could only lead to deeper feelings, and he was never going to allow himself to love or trust another woman again. Not after what had happened with Alisha and Ben.

"I don't know if the medicine is working." His mom rubbed her temple.

"It's the alarm," Sky said. "It's making my ears hurt, too. Are you sleepy? I can help you into bed."

Mom rubbed her eyes. "That would be nice, Elise. You know, I always thought you and my son Jace would make the perfect pair."

Heat covered his face and neck. He stared at a stain in the carpeting.

"Oh?" Sky asked. "What makes you think that?"

"You're both so sweet and darling."

Please stop. Talk about something else. Jace tried sending his thoughts telepathically to his mom.

"My Jace, he's such a sensitive soul. He's a real treasure among the guys."

Jace buried his face into his palms, wishing he could make himself disappear.

"He sounds like a wonderful person." The floor creaked as Sky helped his mom into the bed.

If his skin heated any more, he would burst into flames right there.

"It really is too bad you and he never got together," his mother continued. "But he had to go and marry that Alisha. I never did like her. She's going to break his heart. I just know it."

Jace couldn't look up. How was it his mom could remember his wedding day, but not the fact that it had been the most heartbreaking and humiliating day in his life? Alisha had never even showed up to the church that day.

Sky spoke quietly to his mom. Jace couldn't make out any words over the alarm blaring in the hall. He lifted his head and glanced over at them. His mom nodded, her eyes barely open. Sky held her hand and continued speaking until his mom's eyes closed. After a minute she turned to Jace and gave him the thumbs up.

His skin warmed again, but he raised his thumb.

"Hopefully, she'll be able to sleep through this noise."

"I'm sure she will. She's always been a hard sleeper."

She looked toward the door. "I hope everything is okay out there."

Jace walked over to the window and looked outside. "No emergency vehicles. That's a good sign. Must be something the staff is handling."

"That's a relief." Sky went back to the plush chair. "So, are you really married?"

He held up his ringless left hand. "I'm not my Uncle Bill, either."

"You probably don't have any tea, I'm guessing."

"Nope. I can take you to Sweet Caroline's after this is over, though, if you want." His pulse ran through him like a runaway locomotive. Why had he just offered to do that?

Sky smiled sweetly. "I'd like that."

Jace smiled in return but looked away. What had he

just gotten himself into? He was probably giving her the wrong idea. The last thing he wanted was any romantic involvement. But then again, he'd only offered to buy her tea, not asked her to marry him.

"So, you like taking care of the cottages?" Sky's voice broke through Jace's thoughts.

He glanced up at her. "Yeah. Fixing things seems to be a lost art, and it's kind of nice to help people."

Her pretty brown eyes widened. "I never thought of it like that. It makes total sense."

"So, what do you do?"

"I run a blog."

"For a living?" he asked, surprised. Alisha had kept up a blog when they'd been together, but it had been more like a diary for the world to read.

"Yeah. I get tons of traffic, which in return, pays the bills and then some."

"Huh." He couldn't imagine how that would make any money, but apparently it did. He studied her as she picked up the little dog. Sky was far more than just a pretty face—she was also friendly, smart, and resourceful. Alisha had never made a cent with her blog—in fact, she'd paid all kinds of money to make it exactly how she wanted it.

The alarm went silent as quickly as it had started. Jace waited a minute to make sure it didn't start wailing again, and then he got up and moved the shelf back to its original position. He unlocked the door. "You ready for that tea?"

"Like you wouldn't believe." She twisted her hair into a loose ponytail and stuck the pooch into her handbag.

His breath caught in his throat. He loved that look on her. In fact, it made him want to run his fingers along her jawline—

Stop!

"You okay?" she asked.

"Yeah. My ears are ringing from the silence. Mind if I meet you downstairs by the front door?"

"Sure. I'm going to check on Mark to make sure he's okay after all the excitement." She flicked some loose hair away from her eyes.

How was it that even just that little action made her even more attractive? He needed to get away before he found himself wanting to kiss those luscious lips.

"Okay." He bolted from the room.

NINE

Sky made her way to the Manor's entrance. Mark had been fine and quite appreciative of her checking on him. When she reached the lobby, Jace was speaking with Nurse Gabby on the other side of the desk. Sky went over and leaned on the counter.

"Some excitement, huh?" Gabby asked. The smell of lemon cleaner wafted from her direction.

Sky smiled. "And to think I was expecting a quiet town."

"Oh, you'd be surprised some of the action we get." She winked.

"What was the emergency?" Jace asked, keeping his gaze on a poster of a happy, silver-haired couple behind the nurse.

"One of the patients on the *top floor* got his hands on a knife. It was... well, everything's fine now." She smiled wide, and it seemed forced.

"Is there something special about the top floor?" Sky asked.

Gabby cleared her throat. "That's where our, uh, more challenging residents stay. Some of them have... erm, let's say *special needs*."

"Oh." Sky held her purse, with Pixie in it, closer.

"But you don't need to worry. You need a code to get in and out of that floor. The lock down was just a precaution."

"Good to know. So, is it okay if I bring my dog to visit Mark and Claire again?"

Jace glanced over at her in surprise.

"They both seemed to enjoy Pixie—even though Claire kept calling her Sophie."

Gabby clapped. "Oh, that would be fantastic! You're welcome to talk with anyone on this level who wants to talk with you. It's good to call ahead, though. Just to make sure someone is at the desk to buzz you in."

"Okay." Sky glanced down at the stack of business cards and added the phone number into her contact list. "Will do."

A police officer sauntered down the hallway and stopped at the desk. He leaned against the counter and looked at Gabby, ignoring Jace and Sky. "Everything is secure and all statements have been taken. Someone will need to call the family members of those involved."

"Have a nice afternoon you two." Gabby smiled at Jace and Sky and then turned back to the policeman. "Thank you, Officer Moore. I'll make the calls personally."

Sky waved as she and Jace headed for the door. He held it open for her. She loved that he was such a gentleman. Outside, the warm air and humidity stuck to her. She turned to Jace. "How do you deal with it?"

"With what?"

She pulled her ponytail away from her neck. "The humidity."

"I don't really notice it—not this time of year, anyway. It can be a bit much in the summer. Sometimes I just want to hide inside with the AC all day."

"Well, at least everything is air conditioned."

"And your cottage will soon have a new one, ma'am."

"Please don't call me that."

He stared at her. "What do you mean?"

"Ma'am. It makes me feel old."

"I'm sorry. What do you want me to call you, then?"

"Just Sky is fine."

He nodded. "Okay, Just Sky."

She laughed. "Thanks."

Pixie squirmed in the handbag. Sky pulled her out and set her on the ground. Pixie bounced around, sniffed everything in sight, and then stopped to do her business in the grass.

"You take that dog everywhere?" Jace asked.

"Just about. Even though she has a ton of energy, she behaves whenever we go anywhere."

"That's good, but I don't know how Miss Caroline

will feel about a dog in her shop."

"She probably won't even notice Pixie in my purse. You'll see."

"Huh."

"So, have you lived here your whole life?" Sky asked.

"Yep. Barely ever left, in fact. Is it different than the big city?"

"Oh, definitely. I lived in Seattle for close to ten years, but I grew up in Enchantment Bay, Oregon. It's bigger than here, but still counts as a small town."

"So, you're a small-town girl?" He tilted his head.

"Yeah. When my friend told me about Indigo Bay, I couldn't wait to see it for myself. Having grown up near a bay myself, I figured it had to be a good sign."

"Must be. You tired of the city life?"

"Something like that." If only people didn't mistake her for Aspen all the time, she would love to go back to Seattle. "I guess you could say that you can take the girl out of the small town, but you can't take the small town out of the girl."

"Makes sense." They came to Sweet Caroline's and Jace held the door open for her again.

She scooped up Pixie and put her back into her handbag.

"You going to take your sunglasses off?" Jace asked.

Sky glanced around, making sure those teens weren't in there. They were probably in school. She slid off the glasses and nestled them into a pocket.

They went to the counter and Jace ordered the two teas.

Caroline smiled at both of them. "How are y'all doing today?"

"Good, Miss Caroline," Jace answered. "There was some excitement at the Manor, but everything's fine now."

She tucked some hair behind her ear. "Really? More exciting than last week's shuffleboard tournament?"

"Oh, definitely," Jace said. "You'll have to ask Gabby."

"I certainly will. I'm curious now." She slid the drinks toward them.

Sky reached for her wallet, but Jace handed Caroline enough for both and a tip.

"Thanks," Sky said. "You didn't have to."

"Don't mention it." He took the two drinks from Caroline. "Thanks, Miss Caroline."

"Enjoy." She smiled and then turned to the next customer behind them.

They headed for a table by a window and Jace set the glasses down. He pulled a chair out and looked at Sky. She knew he'd been raised with good manners, but she still couldn't help feeling a little like a princess with him holding doors and chairs for her. She sat. "Thank you."

"Of course." Jace scooted the chair in and then sat across from her. He sipped his tea and glanced out the window.

She took the opportunity to study him, past the obvious—his rugged good looks. Though he didn't say much, his eyes made him seem like there was a lot going in the background. She wanted to figure out what he was thinking about. He seemed like the kind of guy who had some really interesting stories to tell.

He turned his gaze back to her and she looked into his eyes, trying to unravel even just a bit of the mystery that was Jace Fisher.

"You like the tea?" he asked.

"I do. It's very... sweet."

Jace chuckled. "Different than you're used to?"

"Yeah, but I like it." They held each other's gazes, not saying anything. Sky liked how they could slip into a comfortable silence, and not have to fill every moment with talking. "How often do you visit Claire?"

He shrugged. "A few times a week, usually. Probably should stop by more, but she's not usually as with it as she was today."

Sky sipped her drink. "What was different about today?"

"Don't know." He frowned. "Wish I did, though. I'd like more days like today."

"But she still didn't recognize you."

He finished his tea. "Probably too painful. Most everyone she cared about has passed away. I'm just a reminder of that."

Sky patted his hand. "I'm sorry."

Jace's eyes widened and he pulled his hands away. "It happens."

"Still, it has to be hard. Sometimes I wonder if that's why people's minds go when they get older—it's easier to forget than to hurt. I mean, I know it's an actual medical condition, but not wanting to remember could be part of it. I'm not sure I'd want to live with the pain of losing so many people I care about."

"Maybe." He glanced back out the window. A family with two small kids walked by. Jace watched them and frowned.

Sky twisted her ponytail around her hand. Maybe she shouldn't have said anything about it being easier to forget. What if Jace had taken that to mean she thought his mom didn't want to remember him?

"I'm sorry. I shouldn't have said that. Sometimes I speak before I think."

He turned to her, his expression blank. "Come again?"

"About the memories. I know she didn't want to forget you. She seems to have a lot of great ones, and she definitely adores your family. Even if she thinks you're her brother, it's obvious she thinks the world of you from what she said about you."

"It's—" A song sounded across the table. Jace pulled out his phone and looked at the screen. "I have to take this. Pardon me." He turned his back toward her.

"Hello?"

Sky sipped the rest of her tea, guilt wracking her for saying anything about Jace's mom. She finally met a guy who acted like she was normal and she had to let her mouth run off and say something stupid.

Jace turned around. "I'm sorry, but I have to run. A commode is flooding in one of the cottages."

"I understand." Her voice came out smaller than she intended.

TEN

J ace locked his truck and headed for the hardware store. He'd managed to stop the toilet's flooding and dry the floor, but now he had to replace the tubing and the flush valve. His boots sloshed and his pants stuck to his legs as he walked. At least the sun would dry the pants before he got back to the cottages.

"Oh, Jace!" sang Lucille's voice.

He turned to see her waving to him from across the street. She wore the same polka-dotted dress, but this time had her white dog with her.

Jace waved. "Hello, Miss Lucille." He kept walking, hoping she'd take the clue.

The clacking of her heels told him otherwise. He groaned inwardly and pretended not to notice.

"Wait, Jace!"

Sighing, he turned around. "I don't mean to be rude, but I have a commode to fix."

"This will only take a minute."

"Okay."

Lucille looked at her dog. "Sit."

It did as it was told.

Jace noticed that its collar was the exact same shade of bright blue as Lucille's shoes.

"What is it, ma'am?" He adjusted his cap and looked at her.

"I spoke to Maggie and—"

"Maggie?"

"My daughter's niece."

"Right."

"I told her all about you, and she's looking forward to meeting you."

Jace took a deep breath. "I mean no disrespect, Miss Lucille, but I'm really not interested."

"You haven't even met her. Let me show you her picture. Y'all are sure to hit it off."

"It's nothing against you or her. I'm just not interested." He glanced down at his wet pants. "And I really need to get back to the cottages. That commode isn't going to fix itself."

Lucille tilted her head. "Do you have an interest in someone else?"

Sky's lovely face popped into his mind. He thought of the way his pulse had quickened when she had put her soft, smooth hand on his back at the coffee shop. His palms became clammy.

"Do you?" Lucille took a step closer.

"Ma'am, I need to get going." Jace stepped away. "It

was nice talkin' to you."

"I think you're trying to put me off."

"No. I'm just not interested and I have to get back to the cottages and fix that commode before Dallas has my hide."

Lucille stood taller. "Well, I need to make my way over to Frank and Mildred's. They're expecting me."

Jace froze. "Did you say Frank and Mildred?"

"Yes."

His mom had mentioned them. In fact, she'd been convinced Sky was their daughter.

"Are you okay?" Lucille asked.

Jace clenched his fists. It was too much to be a coincidence. Lucille had to have stopped by the Manor and spoken with his mom before lunch.

"Jace?"

He snapped his attention toward her. "Did you talk to my mama?"

"I've chatted with her plenty of times."

"Today." The word almost came out as a growl.

Her eyes widened. "Why, I don't know what you're talking about."

"Don't put ideas in her head. She has enough to deal with. And don't try to set me up with anyone."

Lucille's mouth dropped open. "I beg your pardon?"

"Thank you for understanding." Jace walked away, his mind spinning. *Could* it have been a coincidence that his mom and Lucille both mentioned Mildred and

Frank? It didn't seem likely, especially since the Fishers had never been close to them. On the other hand, if Lucille had been planting ideas in his mom's mind, why not bring Maggie into it? Or had she, and his mom had gotten confused, only remembering Mildred and Frank, since she'd known them? Lucille's great-niece was a stranger to them all.

Not that it mattered now. He'd already set the busybody straight. Jace had no interest in being set up, period. He didn't want to pursue anything with Sky, even though she did set his heart aflutter. Maybe *especially* since the girl in the dark blue cottage evoked such a strong response from him.

He'd sworn never to trust another woman with his heart again. Seeing Alisha with Ben and their two kids outside Sweet Caroline's while Jace had been sitting with Sky may as well have been a message from the heavens above—telling him to keep guarding himself against further hurt.

The hardware store came into view. Good. He needed to focus on toilets and get everything else out of his mind. He didn't want to think about his ex-fiancée, his ex-best friend, some girl named Maggie, and especially not Sky. She was the most dangerous of them all, because she was starting to chip away at the wall he'd built around his heart.

ELEVEN

S ky clicked "publish" and waited as her blog post uploaded for the world. She'd spent the last couple days wandering around town, taking pictures and videos of Indigo Bay as she familiarized herself with everything. In a matter of moments, her followers would know the cute little town as well as she did.

The doorbell rang. She jumped out of her seat, hoping it was Jace. They hadn't seen each other since having tea at Sweet Caroline's a few days earlier. Sky wanted to apologize again for making the thoughtless comment about Alzheimer's. Though she'd been having fun traipsing through town, in the back of her mind, she couldn't stop worrying that she'd offended the handsome handyman.

Instead of Jace, she found a stack of packages.

The mailman turned around and waved. "Have a nice afternoon!"

"You, too!" Sky bent over and slid her fingers underneath the bottom box. Once inside, she set them on the couch and looked at the return address labels. One was a box of clothing, one was beauty products, and the last one was some health food items.

Pixie jumped around, curious.

"Time for some unboxing videos." Sky smiled as she tried to decide which one to open first. One of the best parts of being a fashion and beauty blogger was all the free stuff she got in exchange for reviewing the items.

Pixie barked and then darted around the room.

"Oh, right. I promised you a walk. Let me just put these away first." She lugged the boxes into her room and set them next to the desk, her mind already putting together the videos.

Sky grabbed her phone and the leash, and a couple minutes later, she and Pixie were out in the sand. She was already starting to adjust to the humidity—at least it didn't hit her like a tidal wave when she stepped outside anymore, but she still noticed. With any luck, soon she wouldn't even think about it.

She just enjoyed being outdoors, allowing the sights and sounds of the bay to relax her. They wandered away from the busy part of the beach, stopping every few minutes so Pixie could sniff something and dig around. After stopping about sixty times, they came to a little shaded area underneath the trees. There was even what looked like a seat where a root stuck out at a funny angle.

"This is great, don't you think?"

Pixie just sniffed around at the base of one of the trees.

"I'll take that as a yes." Sky sat on the root and leaned against the tree. "Ah, this *is* nice."

She looped the end of the leash around her foot and watched the water as Pixie explored. Birds flew around, some chasing each other and others floating lazily on the water, bouncing around the soft waves. Eventually, Pixie settled down next to her and curled up.

Sky yawned. "If we stay here any longer, I'm going to fall asleep. But I don't have time for a nap. We need lunch, and then I have to start replying to comments and getting ready for the unboxing videos. Then I have to check the bank account and do a hundred other things. Let's head over to Sweet Caroline's. I'm so not in the mood to make lunch."

She rose, dusted sand off her legs, and grabbed the leash from her ankle, then they made their way back to the cottage. Her stomach growled. She went to the bathroom to check her hair and makeup. When she came out, Pixie was snoring in her doggie bed.

"I'll just let you sleep." Sky rubbed her between the ears and headed back outside. She smiled and waved at people as she took the short walk to the cafe. It was so nice that people were friendly without thinking she was a celebrity.

As soon as she stepped into Sweet Caroline's, Caroline waved to her from behind the counter. "Good afternoon, Sky!"

"Hi, Caroline." She grinned and walked over.

"What can I get you, dear?"

"Do you have the Oceanic sandwich today?"

"Always. It's a staple."

"Perfect. I'll have a whole one with a lemon water."

"Lemon water?" Caroline's mouth dropped. "What, are you on a diet? You're a skinny thing. Have some coffee or tea."

"Thanks, but I just went for a walk. Lemon water sounds divine."

"If that's what you want." She gathered the sandwich onto a plate and added some chips. "So, you made friends with Jace Fisher?"

Sky's cheek's warmed. "I'm not sure I'd say that. We just keep running into each other."

She tucked some hair behind her ears. "Y'all came in to eat together and he paid for your food."

"It was just a glass of tea and I think he was just being nice. I've never met anyone so…" She searched for the right word. "Gentlemanly."

Caroline leaned over the counter and lowered her voice. "Let me tell you something about Jace."

Sky leaned closer. "What?"

"That boy has gone through enough heartache for five people. He barely talks to anyone—and I *never* see him in here with a pretty girl. Or anywhere, for that matter. He fixes the cottages and then hides out."

Sky's heart skipped a beat. "How do you know that?"

"Indigo Bay is a small town, honey. I hear everything that goes on over there in the cottages because my son Dallas owns them. He's Jace's boss."

"Oh, he's the one who doesn't want to replace the AC."

"What?" Caroline tipped her head to the side.

"I have to whack it every couple hours to keep it running. Jace said Dallas hasn't replaced it."

"Oh, honey. I'm so sorry. I'll talk to that boy. He's been distracted with some stuff, but that's no excuse." Caroline glanced behind Sky. "I've got to help some more customers, but I'll talk with Dallas once things slow down around here."

"Wow, I really appreciate that." Sky paid for the food and took it over to a table—the same one she and Jace had sat at the other day—and watched people stroll by outside.

Just as she finished the first half of the sandwich, Caroline came over and sat across from her. "I just spoke with Dallas. He sends his apologies and promises you a new unit as soon as possible."

"Thank you."

"Think nothing of it. You should have a working air conditioner—especially if you're not used to our weather. I hear it's pretty cold up where you come from this time of year."

Sky nodded. "Sometimes I don't put my winter coat away until after the fourth of July."

"I can't imagine. I have a thick coat, but I'm pretty certain it's dusty." Caroline laughed. "I should get back to work, but let me give you some advice about Jace. Just between us ladies."

Sky nearly dropped the glass but recovered quickly. "Okay."

Caroline leaned over the table. "He comes off as tough as nails, but deep down, he's as sweet as they come. Like I said before, life's dealt him some tough cards. I think someone like you is just what he needs to bring him out of his shell."

"You do?"

"I saw the way he was looking at you. But one more thing." Caroline sat taller.

"What?"

"If you think there's any chance he'll end up hurt, walk away now. I just can't imagine what another heartbreak'll do to him."

Sky nodded, deep in thought. "Do you mind telling me what happened?"

"I'm not sure it's my place, but he's had a lot of heartbreak. You know about his mom."

"The poor thing."

"Also, his dad and brother both died."

"What happened?"

"Old age and a work accident—so close together. A

lot of folks think that's what sent poor Claire over the edge."

Sky leaned her elbows on the table and tried to take it all in. "So, Jace is left with no other family?"

"Just some out of town cousins who are twenty years older since it took Claire and Albert so long to have the boys."

Sadness washed through Sky. "That must be so hard for Jace."

"And that's not the all of it, but I don't think it's my place to say more."

Sky nodded, understanding.

Caroline rose and called out a greeting to a family entering the cafe. She turned back to Sky. "I really think you could be good for him. It was so nice to see the way he was looking at you the other day."

"Thanks." Sky couldn't think of anything else to say.

Could she really be the one to help Jace out of his shell? Should she risk the hurt if she moved away? It was too early to tell if she would even stay in town permanently.

TWELVE

Jace hefted the large box out from his truck bed and lugged it over to the front door. He set it on the porch, went back to his truck for the toolbox, and rang the doorbell. He noticed some dark blue paint chipping near the window. He'd have to fix that the next day. Sky shouldn't have to stay in a cottage with peeling paint.

Barking sounded from inside, followed by the deadbolt unlocking. The door opened, and Sky appeared, smiling. Jace's stomach flip-flopped. She was so pretty with her hair hanging down over her shoulders, partially covering a pale purple dress that was just short enough to make his pulse quicken. He quickly looked back up to her stunning eyes.

He cleared his throat. "I've got your AC unit. Sorry it's so late."

She smiled widely. "No problem. I really appreciate you bringing it over after hours."

Jace chuckled nervously. "Nothing's ever off hours for me. If somethin' goes wrong in a cottage at midnight, I show up."

"Well, I don't want to keep you that late. Come on in." She stepped aside.

He set the toolbox inside and picked up the AC box again, pretending it wasn't as heavy as it really was. This one had a bunch of new bells and whistles, and each one seemed to have made it ten pounds heavier.

She closed the door and the little dog danced all around him as he made his way to the living room.

"Pixie, over here!" Sky clapped, and the dog ran over to her.

Jace made his way over to the AC unit and set the box down. He silently caught his breath. "Hey, how long's this been making that clacking noise?"

"It's not supposed to do that?" She sounded surprised.

"No. It sounds like somethin's horribly wrong."

"I didn't know."

He pulled the panel off and shook his head. "It's a good thing we're taking this out. I'm surprised it didn't catch fire."

"What?" Sky exclaimed.

"Yeah, they're not supposed to clack. You really didn't know?"

She shook her head. "I've never had one. You don't need them in Oregon."

"Okay, well, for future reference, they're not supposed to clack."

"Got it. Do you want any help?"

"No thanks." He got to work taking the old air conditioner out. Jace was all too aware of Sky watching, so he tried to push that out of his mind. He just wanted to get the unit installed for her.

A few minutes later, he heard her footsteps moving away from him. He relaxed and worked quicker. Finally, he had it on the floor and was ready to put in the new one. He removed his cap, wiped his forehead, and looked around. Sky sat at the kitchen table, typing on a laptop. Her brows were practically touching and she bit her lower lip.

He didn't use computers much, so he had a hard time imagining what could make her so intense.

She glanced his way, and her expression softened. "Do you want something to drink?"

Jace readjusted his cap. "Sure. That would be great. Thanks."

Her expression lit up. "Do you want a bottle of water or a glass with lemon?"

"Whatever's easiest."

"That's not what I asked. What do you prefer?"

He shrugged. "Surprise me."

"Okay."

Jace pulled his pocketknife from a pocket and broke the seal on the box. He pulled the new unit out and studied it, figuring out the best way to put it in. It was different from all the others, so it might take some extra work.

Sky appeared in front of him, pulling him from his thoughts. He could smell her citrusy perfume. She held two glasses of water, each with a slice of lemon floating on top of ice, and handed him one.

"Thank you." He took it, and their fingers brushed. His breath caught, but she smiled as though the touch was the most natural thing in the world. Jace gulped down the slightly sour water and handed her back the glass. His thumb grazed her finger.

"Want some more?" she asked.

He pulled his hand away and shook his head no. "I should get this installed before it gets too warm in here."

"Let me know if you need anything." She smiled sweetly and walked back toward the kitchen.

Jace released a breath he hadn't realized he'd been holding. He watched her, unable to take his gaze from her feminine curves and walk. He took a deep breath and forced his attention back to the AC unit. The sweet orange scent lingered.

"Are you okay?" she asked.

Pull yourself together. He turned to her and rubbed his hands on his shirt. "Just tryin' to figure out this unit, is all. It's a new model I'm not familiar with yet. I'll be outta your hair before you know it."

"No worries. Take all the time you need." She turned back to the computer and typed so fast it made Jace's head spin.

He brought his attention back to the air condition-er. Once he was able to push everything else out of his mind, he was able to get the unit working in no time. He pushed the power button. Cold air immediately blew out without a sound.

Jace grabbed a rag from his toolbox and wiped some grease from his hands. "Got 'er up and running."

Sky hurried over and stood next to him, checking it out. She stood so close, her soft bare arm touched his. "Oh, that feels great." She held her hands up to the vent with the chilly breeze.

"You're telling me." He cleared his throat and stepped to the side.

She turned to him. "This is going to be great!" Then she threw her arms around him.

Jace stiffened in surprise, but he relaxed, finding the human contact comforting. "It's nothing."

"No, it's not. I hope you know how much I appreci-ate it."

He put his arms around her and patted her smooth back before stepping back. "Glad to help. Well, I'll get this mess out of your living room."

"I can help."

He shook his head. "No, I've got it. Why don't you play around with the AC to make sure you know how to work it before I leave."

"If you're sure."

Jace nodded and returned his tools to the box before

lugging it outside. When he got to the front door, she was putting the AC box into the recycle bin.

"I can take that with me."

"Are you always so polite?" The corners of her mouth twitched like she was holding back a laugh.

"What do you mean?"

"I've got plenty of room in the recycling can. Just have to break down the box."

He gave a little nod and headed back inside to see if there was anything left for him to clean up. In the living room, the AC continued blowing out icy air silently. A show played on the TV, and on the coffee table sat two lemon waters and a bowl of chips. Was she expecting company?

Sky came inside and sat on the sofa. She patted the cushion next to her. "Have a seat."

He froze.

"Come on and relax. My sister sent me a DVD of that new action movie, The Civil Snitch."

"Isn't that still in theaters?"

"Yeah. Aspen has connections."

He'd been wanting to see that movie since he first heard about it. Plus, he couldn't complain about spending extra time with Sky. "Okay."

"Great." She grinned. "Mind getting the lights?"

THIRTEEN

Sky couldn't keep the smile off her face as Jace sat next to her. She'd enjoyed watching him install the air conditioner. He was so intense, taking every step seriously. And as he worked on getting it in, she couldn't help staring as his muscles flexed and bulged with each movement. It made her heart race, just thinking about it.

She took a deep breath, appreciating his masculine, woodsy smell.

"How'd your sister get the DVD?" Jace asked.

Sky considered her wording. The last thing she wanted was for Jace to gain a sudden interest in her because of Aspen. "She works in the industry, and that's one of the perks. She sends everyone in our family free stuff all the time."

"That must be nice."

"Yeah." Sky aimed the remote at the DVD player and pressed play, but nothing happened. She tried a few more buttons. "What am I doing wrong?"

"Here, let me see that."

She handed him the remote. He pressed a few buttons, and loud music blared through the speakers. Jace lowered the volume. "There you go."

"How'd you do that?"

He showed her a complicated series of clicks that she would never remember.

A minute later, the movie started with a guy driving down the freeway, listening to one of Aspen's most popular songs. That was clearly why she'd gotten this particular DVD. An explosion sounded on the screen. Sky jumped and scooted against Jace, hoping he'd put his arm around her.

He didn't.

Gunfire and shouting blared from the speakers. Sky pushed her side into his, nudging his arm. Jace cleared his throat and put his arm around her. It felt good to be so near him, even if he was nervous.

A car chase ensued on screen, and Jace relaxed as he watched. He leaned forward, clearly into it. Police sirens, crashes, and more explosions sounded, drowning out Aspen's song. Finally, the scene calmed down, and the police dragged the main character to jail as he declared his innocence. Jace leaned back against the couch, keeping his arm around Sky.

The movie continued, and eventually, Sky rested her head against Jace's shoulder. He stiffened for a moment, but then slid his hand down to her elbow and gave it a gentle squeeze.

Though Sky wasn't particularly into action movies, she would sit through a movie marathon if it meant sitting there with Jace.

Without warning, Aspen appeared on screen.

Sky's stomach dropped to the floor and crashed through the ground. Her heart raced, waiting for Jace to make the connection. Dread washed through her. She would no longer just be Sky to him. Now she would be Aspen's sister.

Jace turned toward her and looked back and forth between the screen and Sky. "She looks just like you."

Her stomach lurched. She nodded.

"She could be your—"

"Twin." Sky looked down at her turquoise nails. "She is."

Jace paused the show.

"That's your sister? Your *twin* sister?"

Sky nodded, tears threatening. She should've known better than to hope she could get away from Aspen— she'd have to join a tribe in the middle of a rainforest to accomplish that. "Now you know how she got the movie."

"Wait. Is that why you wear sunglasses everywhere in town?"

Sighing, she nodded again. So much for any hope of a plain, normal relationship. In the past, if she hadn't been dealing with someone who wished Sky was Aspen, then she was dealing with liars. She cringed, thinking about her last boyfriend. He'd cheated on her with two different women, and had boldly lied about it the entire time.

Was she doomed to a life of horrible relationships?

Jace's fingertips rested underneath her chin. He guided her to face toward him. She kept her gaze lowered.

"Why don't you want to look at me?"

"Because now everything's different."

"What do you mean?" He sounded confused.

She frowned and looked into his eyes. "Now I'm not just Sky, I'm Aspen Hampton's sister."

"I'm Connor Fisher's brother. Does that change everything, too?" There was a hint of teasing in his voice.

How could she explain the complicated emotions of being Aspen's twin? "People usually obsess over her once they know I'm her sister. Instead of being Sky, I'm Aspen's sister. Some people even pretend I'm her."

"That's crazy." Jace tilted her chin up a little more and held her gaze. He took a deep breath. "You made my heart skip a beat the moment I saw you. That had nothing to do with your twin."

Sky stared at him in disbelief, trying to let his words sink in. "Really?"

He paused and then nodded. "You're sweet, smart, and fun. If there was any doubt, you'd have convinced me when you were so kind to my mama."

Her breath hitched.

"I'd much rather watch a movie or be trapped in a lock down with you than her any day of the week."

She opened her mouth, but couldn't find any words. As his gaze remained locked on hers, he moved closer to her. Her mouth gaped, and the room spun around them. Time seemed to slow as Jace moved his mouth nearer to hers. His lips brushed against hers ever so softly, almost tickling her mouth. His rugged scent intermingled perfectly with the minty taste of his lips.

Jace pulled away with a dazed look in his eyes. He wiped her shimmery gloss from his mouth. "I hope that wasn't too forward. I—"

Sky took his cheeks in her hands, his beard tickling her palms, and pressed a kiss on his lips she was sure to remember for a long time. Jace's eyelashes fluttered shut and his hands found her waist, pulling her closer. Sky closed her eyes and allowed herself to melt into the sweet kiss.

Almost as soon as it had begun, it was over. Jace traced her jawline and then ran a fingertip along her mouth. "We'd best get back to watching that movie."

She gasped for air and nodded. Jace turned the movie back on and put his arm around her shoulder again. Sky leaned against him and relived the kisses in her mind as explosions and gunfire lit up the screen.

FOURTEEN

J ace turned off his alarm and reached for his phone. No jobs around the cottages again. He tossed the phone onto the pillow next to him, placed his hands behind his head, and smiled. The night before had been the best in a long time. He couldn't believe he'd kissed Sky—he certainly hadn't been planning on that. But the wounded expression on her face as she talked about her twin... he'd had to do something to make it better.

He'd worried that kissing her had been too sudden—maybe even unwanted. But then she'd taken the reins and kissed him. He'd never known a kiss could be both sweet and passionate at the same time. But that was Sky's personality. *She* was sweet and passionate. He could see a fire in her eyes, while at the same time she possessed a gentleness that stood in stark contrast to his own jaded personality—except that he didn't feel so jaded this morning.

Jace kicked off the covers and headed for the bathroom, whistling a cheerful tune. It had been a long time since he'd done that—a habit he'd picked up from his dad long ago. He'd stopped after Connor's accident. Then he'd completely fallen apart after the botched wedding.

He pushed all those thoughts aside. They'd held him back long enough. Now he finally had something—someone—to be excited about. He couldn't wait to see Sky again. And since he had no official jobs around the cottages, that gave him the perfect excuse to touch up the paint at the dark blue cottage. He could probably find other things that needed fixing, too. If he was creative enough, he could spend all of his free time making that place as good as it could be.

Once ready, he headed out to his garage and checked his paint cans. Nothing for Sky's cottage. He'd have to head to the hardware store. Jace looked over his supplies to make sure none needed replacing. They were fine. All he needed was the paint. He grabbed his notebook and double-checked the exact shade before heading out the door.

He glanced at his truck, but decided to walk. It wasn't like he was purchasing anything that would be too big to carry. It was a nice morning, and he wanted to enjoy it.

Humming, Jace made his way toward the hardware store. He waved and nodded to everyone he passed. The locals seemed a little surprised—he saw a few raised eyebrows and curious glances exchanged between couples—to see him so chipper. He didn't care.

At the store, he grabbed a can of paint and a few small things he figured he'd need soon. Before long, he was headed back home and his humming had turned back to whistling. He kept returning to Dad's old tunes.

As he neared Sweet Caroline's, he stopped with a couple other people and waited for cars to pass. The woman turned to him.

"Well, Jace! What a surprise."

His stomach twisted. "Alisha."

Ben turned to him. "Hey, there. How've you been?"

Jace stared at them. How could they pretend nothing had happened, when they'd both purposefully destroyed his dreams and humiliated him in one swoop?

"You okay, buddy?"

Jace clenched his fists, squeezing the paint can and the paper bag. "I'm not your buddy, anymore."

"Sorry. I thought we were adults and could move on from the past."

"Move on?" Jace glared at Alisha. "You never showed up to our wedding. I stood there like a fool in front of everyone. Neither one of you could take a minute to give me a heads up?"

Alisha looked away. "Hey, Ben, maybe we should get the kids from your parents. We promised them we wouldn't be gone long."

Jace gritted his teeth. "Yeah, maybe you should."

The three of them exchanged awkward glances.

Jace cleared his throat. "So, why don't you guys tell me what happened? I've always wondered, and I think I deserve some answers."

"It didn't work out." Alisha kept her gaze averted.

"Says you," Jace snapped. "I thought everything was just fine. How long were you two seeing each other behind my back?"

"Hey," Ben said. "It's not like that."

Alisha shook her head. "It wasn't my intention to leave you like that."

"Yet you did—even knowing everything else going on in my life."

She turned and stared at him. "What do you want from me? Ben and I are married now. We have two kids—we're a family. It didn't work out between you and me."

"What do I want?" Jace took a deep breath. "How about answers. All these years, I've been left only *wondering* what went wrong."

Ben took Alisha's hand. "We should get goin', sugar."

"No." Jace stood taller. "You both owe me an explanation. You were my best friend. How could you do this to me? She could've left with some random guy, but she didn't. It was you. What happened?"

Alisha stepped closer to Ben, but kept her gaze on Jace. "Do we have to talk about this here?"

"It's as good a place as any," Jace snapped. "Or

would you rather sit down at Sweet Caroline's over tea?"

"Fine." She glared at him. "You changed, Jace. A lot. I thought our love would be enough, but then I saw it wasn't."

"So, you decided to add to everything I'd already been through? My father died of old age, my brother was killed at work, my mama couldn't remember me, and you decided to top off my year with leaving me at the altar. That makes a lot of sense."

"Jace, we were bickering a lot. Don't you remember that?"

"I do," Ben said.

"Who asked you?" Jace glared at him.

Ben rolled his eyes. "You said you wanted to know what happened. Alisha felt abandoned and lonely because you weren't paying her enough attention. We got to talking, and one thing led to another."

"So, you slept with my fiancée?"

"No." Ben's brows came together. "We realized *we* had a lot more in common than you two, but we also knew that everyone would despise Alisha around here, so we packed a couple bags and headed north to stay with my grandparents."

"Why do you even care anymore?" Alisha asked. "It was so long ago."

"This summer will be four years."

"Oh, my word." She covered her mouth.

"What?" Jace demanded.

"You never moved on, did you?"

Ben gave Jace a double-take. "Are you still stuck on Alisha?"

"No, actually I'm not. Doesn't mean I don't want answers."

"You were too much of a downer for her." Ben's brows came together. "*That's* your answer. Nobody wanted to be around you with all your moping and complaining."

"Unbelievable." Jace turned to Alisha. "We'd been together since we were fourteen. You left me because I wasn't fun after my life crumbled down around me?"

"We grew apart, Jace."

"Whatever you have to tell yourself so you can sleep at night."

Her mouth dropped open. "Are you serious?"

Ben narrowed his eyes at Jace. "Time to move on with your life, buddy. We're moving back, so it would be best for everyone."

"You mean you."

"We'll see you around." Ben stepped away, pulling Alisha's arm.

Lucille walked over with her dog. "What's going on around here? An unhappy reunion?"

"I was just leaving," Jace said.

"Oh." Lucille looked at Jace. "I wanted to discuss that blind date with Maggie."

"That's a great idea," Alisha said. "Help him to finally get over me. Let's go, Ben."

Jace glared at her. If looks could kill…

"Are you free a week from Thursday?" Lucille asked.

"No," Jace said quickly.

"He's lying, Miss Lucille," Alisha said with a song to her voice. She and Ben walked around the corner.

Lucille smiled. "So, next Thursday?"

"Actually, next *never* works better for me."

"Alisha's right. It's high time you move on and find yourself a sweet girl, like my Maggie."

"I already—"

"Bernadette!" Lucille called, looking behind Jace and waving. She turned back to Jace. "I have to talk with her about the upcoming charity gala. Press your best clothes by Thursday." She ran off, her heels clacking on the sidewalk.

"I'm *busy!*"

FIFTEEN

Sky uploaded her latest video and turned to Pixie. "Wanna go to the pet store?"

Pixie ran around in circles, barking. Not that she knew they were going to Happy Paws, she just got excited whenever Sky said, 'Wanna go?'

Sky glanced in the mirror on her desk, flattened her hair, and fixed her lipstick—just in case she ran into Jace. He *did* work at the cottages. She sighed dreamily, remembering the night before. Her insides turned to mush as she relived the kiss… again. Not only did he prefer her to Aspen, but he was perfect—gorgeous without being conceited, mysterious without being a jerk, and strong without being intimidating.

How on earth was he still single? It was best not to question a good thing.

Pixie barked, bringing Sky back to the present.

"Right. The pet store. Wanna pick out a new toy?"

The cute little pup danced in another circle. Sky double-checked her hair and makeup before getting up.

She grabbed her good camera, hoping the Montgomerys wouldn't mind her taking some photos of their shop for her blog. Her readers couldn't get enough of Sky's pictures of Indigo Bay. She'd spent hours replying to comments asking for more.

Just as Sky clipped on Pixie's leash, her phone rang. Excitement buzzed through her. Maybe it was Jace. She dug the phone out of her purse, and her mouth dropped when she saw the caller ID.

She accepted the call. "Aspen?"

"Hey, sis! How's it going?"

"I'm a little surprised." Sky almost never heard from her twin aside from the social media updates she posted to the world. "Congrats on being in the movie."

"You watched it," Aspen squealed. "It was so hard not to tell you guys. I wanted everyone to be surprised. Now I'm a singer *and* an actress! Mom and Dad were beside themselves."

"Congratulations."

"So, how's that little town you're in?"

Sky arched a brow. She hadn't told Aspen about her move. "Did Mom and Dad tell you?"

"No, silly. I follow your blog."

"You do?" Sky asked, surprised.

"I gotta keep up with my kid sister somehow, right?"

"Still hanging onto being three minutes older?"

"You know it, baby sis. Well, I have to get going. I'm going to be in a beer commercial. Just wanted to call and let you know I love you. I know I'm busy all the time, but family is first in my heart."

Sky didn't know how to respond. Part of her felt guilty for hating the effects of being Aspen's twin, but she also loved hearing that she was still important.

"You still there?" Aspen asked.

"Yeah. I love you, too."

"Gotta go. I'll try to make it down to North Carolina one of these days."

"South Carolina."

"Right. Love ya!"

"You, too."

The call ended. Sky took a deep breath and watched Pixie chewing on a toy.

"Wanna go?"

She jumped up and wagged her tail furiously.

Sky grabbed her big sunglasses from the table next to the door and slid on a denim bucket hat. The hat and glasses probably made her stick out more, but she didn't care. So far, no one other than those girls at Sweet Caroline's had mistaken her for Aspen.

Once out in the humidity, Sky headed for her car for the air conditioning. Then she stopped. "No. I need to get used to this."

She and Pixie headed for Happy Paws Pet Shop, saying hello to those they passed. A few stopped to pet Pixie, who of course adored the attention.

Finally, they made it into the adorable—and more

importantly, air conditioned—shop. Sterling was busy painting a brown, curly-furred Labradoodle on the front window. He wiped his forehead, smearing paint on it. "Hi, there. Sky, is it?"

She nodded, removed her sunglasses, and glanced at the window. "Nice artwork."

"Thanks. I went to art school, and this is the only way I get to use my skills."

"I heard that," Violet called. She appeared from around the corner and laughed. "Don't listen to him. He draws and paints more than he does anything else."

"Hey, now." Sterling laughed and went back to painting.

"Can I help you find anything?" Violet set down a bag of dog food nearly as big as she was.

"Pixie's going to pick out a toy, and I need to get some more food for her, but I have a question for you that's going to sound crazy."

"You're in luck," Sterling said. "She loves crazy."

Violet shook her head. "Because I'm married to you, right?"

Sky laughed. "You walked into that one."

"Guess I did."

"So," Violet said. "What's the crazy question?"

"I was hoping I could take pictures of your shop. It's adorable, and I have a popular blog. My readers will love it, and who knows, maybe it'll help bring extra business."

"Hold your horses." Violet smiled widely. "You want to give us free advertising?"

"Uh, basically, yeah. You don't mind?"

Violet turned to Sterling. "Hey, honey. I think I found my new best friend."

Sky laughed. "We all win."

"Let me just dust a few things off while you get the toy and dog food. 'Kay?"

"Sure." Sky took Pixie over to the toys and set a few in front of her. Pixie sniffed and poked at them until finally taking one in her mouth. Then she headed over to the food aisle, grabbed a bag of Pixie's favorite, and took it all to the counter.

"All done." Violet dropped a rag behind the counter.

"Let me pay for these first."

"Are you kiddin'?" Violet shook her head. "No way. Take 'em. It's the least we can do."

Sky frowned. "I can't do that."

"Sure you can. We can't afford to pay you for advertising, but we can afford this."

"But this isn't really an ad. It's just a feature. I—"

"No arguing. Get those pictures taken before I have to dust again."

"Okay." Sky pulled out her camera and planned to leave some cash by the register before leaving. She snapped pictures of the cute displays of toys, even getting a few of Sterling painting and one of Violet dressing a stuffed dog in a football jersey for a display.

Time flew by as she captured over a hundred images.

Just before she finished, another customer came in. Sky tiptoed toward the register to slip the money for her purchase.

"Hi, Miss Lucille," Sterling said. "How are you and Princess today?"

"Couldn't be better." The older blonde woman in a flowered, puffy dress smiled at him. "I got some new shoes, so Princess needs a collar to match."

Sky arched a brow. That was certainly something she'd never heard of before—and Sky was known for overdressing her pup. She slid the fifty underneath a stapler and headed for the front door. The two dogs sniffed each other. Both had bows on their heads, and sure enough, the white dog's collar matched her owner's magenta pumps.

The older woman paid no attention to Sky or Pixie. She turned to Violet. "Remember my great-niece, Maggie?"

Violet nodded. "Is she enjoying her stay?"

"She's talking about staying all summer, though if I have my way, she'll move here. Oh, and I even set her up on a date."

Sky waved to Sterling and Violet, then opened the door.

"Jace Fisher is going to take her out on the town

next Thursday."

Sky froze in place. *Jace* was going on a date with that woman's niece?

Lucille continued. "Maggie's going to show him a good time and finally pull that boy from his shell."

Head spinning, Sky stepped outside before she could hear any more about Jace seeing someone else.

SIXTEEN

Jace dropped the paint and the bag on the floor and stormed over to the kitchen. Then he marched into his bedroom. He paced, unable to think straight.

Hadn't Ben and Alisha done enough to ruin his life? Why did they have to encourage Lucille to set him up with Maggie?

Actually, now that Jace thought about it, they *hadn't* ruined his life. They'd done him a favor. If Alisha was really that shallow, he could only imagine how miserable he would be married to her. Not to mention having a cheating lowlife for a best friend.

But that didn't stop the anger. It pulsated through him. He wanted to break something, but that wouldn't accomplish anything. It would just give him something to clean up.

He paced through every room, fuming. How had the day made such a drastic turn? He'd woken up so happy he'd actually whistled. Whistled! Now he felt stupid for allowing himself happiness and hope.

Maybe he was an idiot for getting excited about Sky. It had been one good evening, and two quick kisses. She may have even woken up having forgotten all about it.

Why did he have to run into Alisha, Ben, and Lucille? Was it just life's way of reminding him that he didn't deserve to be happy?

Jace spun around, and before he knew it, his fist went through the wall. He pulled his hand back and shook it out, staring at the hole. Great. Now he'd have to fix that before Dallas saw it. But first, he needed to get outside. If he stayed there, he would only wind up with more holes in the drywall to repair.

His phone rang. He couldn't talk to whoever it was—probably Dallas needing something done at one of the cottages. That would have to wait. Without looking at his phone, he threw it on his bed. He needed to calm down.

He grabbed his sketchbook and pencils. That would be a much better way to work out his emotions. Jace stormed outside and headed for his favorite spot between the trees. The best thing about it was that no one else knew about it. In all of his times there, he'd never run into anyone else.

Once comfortable on the root seat, he leaned against the trunk and studied the scene before him. Despite the beautiful beach, all he could see was Alisha, Ben, and Lucille. Thankfully, they weren't actually there. If they were, Jace would be tempted to do what he'd done to the wall to Ben's smug face.

He closed his eyes and listened to the waves rolling onto the shore, birds squawking, and the sounds of kids in the distance. The children only reminded him of Alisha and Ben's family. Not that Jace cared anymore. Those two deserved each other.

Taking a deep breath, he opened his eyes. He needed to get his mind off everything, and the only way to do that was to start drawing. He pulled out a pencil, not even paying attention to what color it was, and started drawing the waves. They were orange, but he didn't care. They could be blood red for all it mattered.

Time disappeared as he drew the scene before him in a strange array of colors. In a way, he liked it—the orange water, the purple sand, the green sky, and pink birds. He continued picking colors at random as he added more to the drawing. He was about to finish it off with yellow kids in the distance when footsteps sounded.

Jace froze. He *never* heard that in his spot. Had someone finally found it? He quickly shoved his art into the bag before anyone could see it. His heart sank as he looked over. Then shock took over. "Sky?"

She stood there without her dog. Her eyes widened and her mouth dropped, her expression registering the same surprise he felt. Then her face twisted, almost as though disgusted.

"How'd you find this place?" Jace slid his yellow

pencil and the sketch pad into his bag.

"I found it the other day. Pixie and I have been coming out here to get space."

Well, if anyone had to find it, at least it was her. He moved over and patted the space on the root next to him.

She folded her arms and didn't budge.

"I tried calling. Are you ignoring me?"

"No. I left my phone at home."

Her eyes narrowed, almost like she was trying to figure out if he was telling her the truth.

"I come out here when I need to get away from everything."

Sky's mouth formed a straight line.

"You okay?" he asked, pretty sure he already knew the answer.

"Not really."

"That makes two of us, then. Wanna talk about it?"

She opened her mouth and then closed it. Then she started to say something, but then stopped.

"Or you can just sit." He patted the root again.

"I thought last night was special." She sounded angry.

"So did I." Jace wanted to say more, but given that she looked as pissed as he felt, he didn't dare. They'd probably end up in an argument, and she was the last person he wanted to be at odds with. They stared at each other for a full minute.

"Are you seeing anyone else?" she demanded.

He gave her a double-take. "What? No. I meant every word I said last night."

"Then why did someone in town say you're going out with a Maggie?"

Suddenly, everything made sense. Anger ran through him, blurring his vision.

"What's going on?" Sky exclaimed.

Jace took a deep breath and looked at her. "Lucille, Indigo Bay's very own busybody, has it in her mind that her great-niece Maggie and I would make a perfect couple—despite the fact I keep telling her I'm not interested."

"She's convinced you're taking Maggie out on Thursday."

"Then both she and Maggie will be sorely disappointed. The only person I have any interest in dating is standing right in front of me."

Sky held his gaze, her expression slowly softening. "Really?"

He nodded. "Ask anyone in town, I haven't been on a date in years. That's why Lucille has decided to turn me into her personal project. Her timing is spectacularly horrible."

Sky threw her arms around him and squeezed tight. He wrapped his arms around her, and his entire body relaxed. The fruity aroma of her hair relaxed him further. "I'm really sorry about the misunderstanding."

"It's not your fault. Why won't that lady listen to you?"

Jace shrugged. "I guess she has it in her mind, and she doesn't want anyone getting in the way."

"She bragged about your date with Maggie to the Montgomerys. I don't know if she's telling anyone else."

He clenched his jaw. "Oh, I'm sure she is. I'm going to have to put a stop to this." He pulled back and stared into Sky's eyes. "I know we haven't known each other that long, but I want to make sure you know everything I said before is the truth. Do you believe me?"

Sky held his gaze for a moment before nodding yes.

SEVENTEEN

Sky threaded her fingers through Jace's. He tried to pull away. That's when she noticed his knuckles were cut. She squeezed his hand. "Are you okay? What happened?"

"It, uh, I was just being careless. It's nothing."

"We should get you cleaned up."

"I'll be fine. I should find Lucille and set her straight. Can't have half the town thinking I have eyes for anyone other than you."

"Don't worry about it. I learned a long time ago that it does nothing to worry what anyone else thinks."

"Yeah, but—"

"Let's *show* them why you don't have any interest in Maggie. Something that busybody won't be able to ignore."

Jace raised an eyebrow. "What do you have in mind?"

"We need to be seen together—everywhere. Holding hands. Laughing together." She paused. "Kissing."

The corners of Jace's mouth twitched. "You mean like this?" He leaned in and brushed his lips across hers.

She smiled. "Exactly."

He held her gaze. "Maybe we should practice that again."

"Probably should." She pressed her mouth on his and took in his scent. He smelled like the beach and the salty air.

Jace put his hands on the small of her back and pulled her close. He started to deepen the kiss, but then pulled back, worry in his eyes. "This is moving pretty fast, isn't it? Are you sure this is what you want?"

Sky nodded, staring deep into his eyes. They seemed lighter out on the beach—almost a blue-green color. She could get lost in them if she wasn't careful. Sky pulled back and focused on his entire face. "I know we just met last week, but I really want to get to know you better. You're a man of many mysteries, and I respect that. I'm not going to be one of those girls who demands you spill all. Tell me what you feel comfortable with, and I promise to treasure it forever."

Jace pulled her close and wrapped her in a strong, warm embrace. "How can you be so wonderful?"

She leaned her head on his shoulder. "Easy. I know when I've found something special. To be cheesy and take a line from my favorite movie, you're a diamond in the rough."

"You like *Aladdin?*" he asked.

"I probably watched it a thousand times as a kid."

"Really? I used to want a monkey because of Abu."

Sky laughed. "So did I. Aspen wanted a genie to grant her wishes, but I just wanted a moody monkey."

"You may have gotten that in the form of me."

She shoved him. "You're no monkey."

"I can think of a few people who might disagree with you." His mouth quivered as he obviously held back a laugh.

"Who cares what they think?" Sky stepped back and took his hand again. "We should get that cleaned up and then head out and show this town exactly who Jace Fisher digs."

"Digs? Do people still say that?" His voice held a teasing tone.

"I just did. Come on." She pulled on him. He grabbed his bag, and she dragged him to her cottage. Pixie ran around in circles and jumped on them. "Down, girl! I've got a first aid kit in the bathroom. Do you want help?"

"Nah, I got it." He went into the main bathroom and closed the door.

Sky sank onto the couch and patted her knees. Pixie jumped onto her lap and licked her face. Sky rubbed the soft fur and released a sigh. She was exhausted from the range of emotions she'd just experienced—everything from anger to elation. Pixie kept kissing her, so Sky set her on the floor. The pup jumped right back up.

Sky laughed. "You're persistent."

Pixie sat and licked a paw.

"You okay in there?" Sky called to Jace.

"Fine," he called back.

Sky ran her hands down Pixie's back. "I think I'm falling hard, Pix. I didn't want to fall in love again, but it's happening and I don't feel like fighting it."

The little Yorkie yapped happily.

"It's a risk," Sky continued. "But it's worth it this time. He isn't like most guys—in the best way possible." She paused, thinking about her botched relationships. It wasn't just the serial cheater. The one before him had lied about a gambling addiction. Sky hadn't found out about that until after he'd lost hundreds of her dollars. He'd told her it was to fix his car. Jace would never do anything like that. He was trustworthy.

The bathroom doorknob jiggled. Sky picked up Pixie and jumped to her feet. Jace came out with some bandages wrapped around his knuckles.

"Where do you want to go first?" She felt as bouncy as the excitable pup in her arms.

He shrugged. "Depends. What are you in the mood for? Tea? Lunch? A stroll?"

"How about all of the above?"

"At the same time?" Jace tilted his head.

She nodded.

"I don't follow."

"I have an idea." She set Pixie down, washed her

hands, and pulled her picnic basket from one of the cupboards.

"Go for a walk and then eat somewhere?" Jace asked.

"How does the park sound? I've been wanting to spend some time there. It's so cute."

"Sure." He stepped into the kitchen. "What can I help with?"

Sky's heart warmed. "Grab some sandwich fixings from the fridge."

He did, and she slipped a bottle of wine and some chocolates into the basket—her favorite treats. Together they made the lunch and headed outside.

"You mind if Pixie comes along?" she asked.

"I wouldn't have it any other way. And I'm not letting you carry that basket." He took it from her.

Sky thought her heart might literally explode with happiness. He was a true gentleman, and combined with his southern charm, it was almost enough to send her soaring into the air. Could he be any more perfect?

They walked down the street with Pixie, and they smiled at everyone they saw. Sky looped her arm through his so there wouldn't be any mistake. Anyone who heard Lucille's story about her niece would be forced to give it a second thought.

Maybe it would even teach that woman to stop meddling in people's lives.

They reached the town park. It had a charming gazebo with lights, and in the distance was more beach—half of Indigo Bay seemed to be beach. Lifeguards sat at their posts, spread evenly apart.

Jace adjusted his cap over his eyes to block the sun and looked around. "The gazebo is free if you want to eat there, or we can pick something in the sun if you prefer."

"I'm still adjusting to this humidity. Do you mind if we take one of the tables in the shade?"

"Not at all." They walked toward some trees off to the side. Jace set down the basket and pulled out the food. Once it was all set out, he pulled out the bottle of wine. "When did you sneak this in?"

She tried to hold back a smile. "When you weren't looking. Hope you don't mind."

"That a beautiful and sweet woman wants to share wine with me? Do I look crazy to you?"

Heat crept into her cheeks. "Nope." Sky dug into the basket until she found the corkscrew. She handed it to him and pulled out the wine glasses. Yes, she was falling hard—and fast.

EIGHTEEN

J ace sipped his wine, enjoying both the relaxation it allowed him and the sight before him. Sky popped a piece of chocolate into her mouth and smiled, fluttering her lashes. His stomach flip-flopped. He wasn't used to anyone having such an effect on him.

It was hard not to think back to Alisha—the only other person he had ever felt that way about before. That hadn't ended so well. His internal protection system sounded sirens, warning him he was in danger-ous territory.

He shoved them aside. Sky wasn't Alisha, and the situations were completely different. When he'd gotten together with Alisha, they'd been fourteen. Jace hadn't even started shaving yet. They had been young and immature.

Alisha had been right about one thing earlier, though. Jace *had* ignored obvious signs—he hadn't wanted to think they'd grown apart. It'd been comfort-ing to be with the same person for ten years, and even more so thinking about spending the rest of their years together. But convenience didn't make for a good relationship.

He studied Sky as she spoke about her childhood. Her eyes lit up and her hands moved around as she described things. Pixie jumped up onto the bench next to her, and watched, her head moving back and forth as if watching a tennis match. Sky had such a zest for life, and it was contagious. Jace had spent the last several years just existing. He'd thought that it was better than opening himself up to hurt again.

Now he doubted that. He wanted what she had, and hopefully, spending time with her was exactly what he needed—he wanted that to be what he needed.

Sky leaned her elbows on the table and studied him. "So, what about you? What was your childhood like?"

He stiffened. Panic ran through him. What was he supposed to talk about? All of his happy memories were tainted with the deaths of his dad and brother, and the fact that his mom couldn't remember him. He certainly couldn't talk about his teen years—they were all filled with Alisha as the center of his world.

Sky's expression clouded slightly. "It's okay. We can talk about something else. Like the—"

"No, I can tell you about my life growing up." His mind raced for a safe memory, maybe something as light-hearted and carefree as she'd just shared. "My brother and I used to run around town, getting into all kinds of mischief. We thought we were international spies for a while, and Conner convinced me everyone in town was hiding top secret information from the president." Jace chuckled and shook his head. "In fact, I overheard the mayor speaking about something to one of the ladies from the Ashland Belle Society. I confronted him, and boy howdy, he was madder than a wet hen."

A slow smile spread across Sky's gorgeous face. "Oh, no."

Jace nodded. "It didn't go over well for me or Connor. Our dad tanned our hides like never before. We never played spies after that."

Sky covered her mouth. "That's awful."

He shrugged. "That's what we got for meddling with the mayor. Certainly not our best idea, but we learned to be more careful with our antics."

"Sounds like you two were best buds."

"We really were." Sadness washed over Jace. It'd been a terrible hit when Connor had been killed. What made it even worse was how sudden it was—and so soon after Dad's passing.

She opened her mouth, and then closed it. Guilt stung at Jace for making things so hard on her, but he couldn't bring himself to opening up and telling her everything. Not yet, anyway. Hopefully, she would be willing to wait around until he could tell her more. He wanted to say something, but everything was so convoluted. Where would he start that he didn't have to explain everything in his life?

Several beats passed before Sky spoke. "People always think that Aspen and I were inseparable, but really we weren't. I mean, it wasn't like we didn't get along or anything. We just aren't an extension of each other, like people think twins should be."

"I got that feeling." He wanted to say more, to talk about his family, but the words wouldn't come. As much as he wanted to trust her, he just couldn't. It was likely a matter of time before he opened up, but that was exactly it—he needed the time.

"Family can be tough." Sky gave him a sad smile. It was almost like she was telling him that she understood his struggle.

"It sure is. Complicated, too."

"I couldn't agree more." She reached across the table and slid her hand in his. "We don't have to talk about that. Do you want to walk around town or the beach?"

Jace didn't really care what they did as long as they were together. She was the first person in such a long time that he'd actually enjoyed spending time with, and he couldn't get enough of her. He'd have agreed to just about anything. "Whatever you want to do."

He picked up their trash and took it over to the bin. When he returned, she had most everything else returned to the picnic basket already. He helped her with the rest and grabbed the basket.

She laced her fingers through his again. Oh, how he loved that simple gesture. His hands felt so large and rough against hers. Warmth ran through him that had nothing to do with the springtime weather. They walked along the path to the sidewalk and headed toward the cottages.

Jace hoped that everyone in Indigo Bay saw them together. He wanted to shout from the rooftops that he was falling in love again, this time with the most beautiful and kindhearted woman alive. Instead, he turned to her and smiled, hoping the intensity of his eyes said what he couldn't get his mouth to say.

She smiled back and squeezed his hand. Did that mean she got the message? He'd been out of the dating game so long, he wasn't sure he knew what he was doing. He squeezed her hand back, determined to do everything right this time.

NINETEEN

Sky replied to the last blog comment and closed her laptop. Her fans had loved the post about the Happy Paws Pet Shop. She'd focused not only on the adorable setup, but also their line of pet fashion. They had coats, shirts, hats, and even pajamas for dogs. It was the perfect combination for her fans—pet-loving fashionistas.

As usual, there were some hecklers. The more popularity her blog gained, the more came out. The online trolls always found something to complain about. This time, they were saying that animals shouldn't be kept as pets for people's entertainment. Sky didn't even have to respond because her followers had already jumped in and put the haters in their place.

She stretched and rose from her chair. Her legs ached from sitting for so long. She really needed to invest in a standing desk or maybe even a treadmill desk considering how much time she spent in the chair. That was something on her list to do after she found a place to settle, and the more time she spent with Jace, the more she wanted to stay in Indigo Bay.

Her heart fluttered just thinking about him. It had been a few days since their picnic, and she'd only seen him in passing for a moment. A pipe had burst in one of the other cottages, leaking and causing flooding. Jace had been dealing with that, repairing the leak and preventing further water damage.

He'd been pretty stressed when she'd run into him, so she gave him space to focus on his job. It sounded like it would take a lot of time and effort to get the whole thing taken care of. She'd offered to bring him some food, but he said he was fine.

It might even be a good thing that they had the time apart. He'd mentioned that things were moving fast between them. Sky didn't mind personally—she was used to a faster pace of life than everyone in Indigo Bay. Probably from her time living in Seattle. When she'd returned to her hometown of Enchantment Bay, things had felt slow.

She glanced at her phone. She'd been inside the cottage for the last two days. It was time to get outside and have some actual human interaction. She loved talking with her blog followers, but there was something special about actually talking with someone in person, face-to-face. Besides, maybe she would run into Jace.

If she were being honest with herself, that was the main reason she wanted to head out. Sky tried to remember which cottage he'd said had the water problems, but it escaped her.

"Wanna go for a walk?" she called out, not sure where Pixie was hiding. Little skittering footsteps sounded from the direction of the sliding glass door. Pixie appeared and crashed into Sky's legs. "Watching the ducks again?"

That had become the pup's favorite pastime activity other than sleeping.

"Give me just a minute to freshen up." Sky went into the bathroom and looked in the mirror. She didn't look bad for a non-video recording day, but she didn't want to look *not bad* if she ran into Jace.

Sky turned on her curling iron and fixed her makeup while it heated. She curled a few locks and then ran her fingers through it, giving it a nice wave around her face. Once she was satisfied, she practiced her smile a few times.

Pixie was by the back door again, watching the ducks. Her head moved back and forth, following one of the ducklings in particular.

The doorbell rang. Sky's heart skipped a beat, hoping it was Jace, but she knew better. The mail always came this time of day, and she was expecting several packages.

Pixie barked and ran for the front door, the birds completely forgotten. Sky opened the door, saw the pile of boxes, and called a thanks to the mailman, who waved as he climbed back into his truck.

She squatted to pick them up when she noticed the bush to her left had been cut back. Leaving the boxes, she stepped onto the grass, the cool blades tickling the soles of her feet, and studied the shrub. It wasn't her imagination. The plant had been trimmed significantly, and it looked a lot better.

Something else was different, but she couldn't quite place what. Sky put her hands on her hips and studied the side of the cottage. The paint—it had been chipped near the window, but now it was flawless. She couldn't even remember where the paint had been chipped.

Her heart warmed, spreading throughout from head to toe, feeling like a warm embrace.

Jace had done all that work, but when?

Pixie pranced out and sniffed the grass.

Sky scooped her up and hugged her. "Look what Jace did for us, Pix."

The pup licked her cheek. Sky rocked her back and forth, staring at the shrub and new paint. He'd been thinking about her, and as tired as he had to be, he'd gone to the effort of making her cottage nicer—though it had been just fine before. He didn't often say much, but this gesture spoke volumes.

She set Pixie down, who scampered back inside. Sky grabbed the boxes, which felt as light as air, and she headed inside, unable to feel the ground beneath her feet.

TWENTY

Jace brushed off dirt from his arm as he walked away from the red cottage. It seemed like each one had its own catastrophe, one after the other. If it wasn't plumbing, then it was something else. The resident in the red cottage had been convinced animals were living in the walls. He had looked around for where they might have made themselves at home, but found nothing in the walls or under the house—as he'd expected. However, something had gotten into the garbage and strewn it all over the yard. Once Jace had cleaned up the mess, he had to fix the lid so the critters wouldn't be able to get it open.

He caught a glimpse of his reflection in a window of the turquoise cottage as he walked by. He had flecks of dirt all through his hair, dark circles under his eyes, and a streak of mud and who-knew-what-else smeared across his forehead. His clothes weren't in any better shape. Worse, actually. He'd have to toss the ripped pants.

Jace switched the toolbox to his other hand and

picked up his pace as he headed home. He couldn't wait to get cleaned up and then hopefully sleep for a full day—that is, if none of the other cottages had any disasters that needed to be taken care of immediately.

Finally, his place came into view. His eyes grew heavier at the thought of being so close to his bed.

Barking sounded not far away. It sounded familiar.

"Jace!" came Sky's voice.

His stomach tightened. As much as he wanted to see her—the days felt like weeks since their picnic—but he didn't want her to see him all grimy and gross. He'd probably repulse her.

He turned around and gave a little wave. His heart felt like it would jump into his throat. "Hey there, Sky."

She grinned and ran over to him, seeming not to notice that he was covered in filth. She was the exact opposite of him, wearing a cute—clean—red sundress and had a new wave to her shiny hair. "Thanks so much for fixing the chipped paint and cutting back the bushes. It looks amazing."

A thrill ran through Jace. She'd noticed. "I just wanted it to be nice for you."

"Nice? It's great. I can't believe you did that when you have so much other stuff to take care of."

He shrugged. "I had a break between emergencies."

"Still, you could've rested, but you didn't."

"I'm glad you like it. Now that it looks like I have a break from work, maybe we can go on a date when you're free? I'd like to take you somewhere nice. There's a restaurant called Figaro's I've heard good things about." It would also cost about a week's worth of pay, but it'd be worth every penny. "I would—"

She threw her arms around him and squeezed tight. Jace hesitated, not wanting to get her dirty, but he could already see dust and dirt smearing onto her perfectly tanned shoulders. He wrapped his arms around her and rested his hand on her upper back, careful not to touch the dress.

Sky stepped back and gazed at him like he was some kind of hero.

Jace didn't know why she was looking at him like that, but he couldn't help basking in it. He also felt the need to say something. But what? His mind went blank from the pressure. Then he noticed the smudges on her outfit. "Your dress. I didn't mean to get it dirty."

She glanced down. "I'm not worried about it. That's why they make stain sprays."

"Still, I feel bad."

"Then take me out to dinner to make up for it." Her nose crinkled as she grinned at him.

She was breathtaking. He struggled to find his voice. "Friday night?"

"Works for me. I'll let you get going. What time should I be ready for our date?"

"I'll call you after I make the reservations."

"Sounds great." Sky took a step near him and

pressed her soft lips on his. She smelled of apples and mint. He, on the other hand, reeked of coons and standing water. Not that she seemed to notice. She brushed something off his cheek and smiled sweetly. "I'll be waiting."

Jace watched as she strolled away. He tried to walk back to his home, but couldn't get his feet to cooperate until Sky had rounded a corner and was out of sight. He rubbed the spot on his face she'd touched and took in the whole interaction, still surprised that she hadn't been bothered by his appearance.

As his home came into view, his phone rang. He groaned, knowing by the ringtone that it was his boss calling. Reluctantly, he reached for it and accepted the call. "Hello, Dallas."

"Jace, the purple cottage has a hornet nest on the roof and they say the bees are flying around the front door so they can't get out."

"Okay." Jace turned around. "I'll have to stop by the store and pick up some insecticide spray." He'd also need some protective netting to keep from getting stung. "Tell them to stay away, and I'll take care of it in no time."

"Will do." The call ended.

Jace's body ached and his eyelids grew heavy. It was feast or famine around the cottages, and he couldn't wait for the famine. He thought about heading back home to brew some coffee, but it'd be quicker to stop by

Sweet Caroline's on the way. She knew how to make it much stronger than Jace did, anyhow.

He kicked his feet on the sidewalk before getting to the cafe and shook as much caked-on grime from his clothes as he could. No sense in giving the poor woman more work to do by leaving a trail of dirt in his wake.

"Hi, Jace," Caroline greeted him. "Looks like my boy is keeping you busy these days."

"Yes, ma'am. All the cottages seem to have something going wrong lately. Could I get a cup of your strongest coffee to go, please?"

"Sure thing, and this one's on the house."

He gave her a double-take. "Are you sure?"

She grabbed a white paper cup and poured black coffee inside. "It's the least I could do. You keep the resort running."

"I wouldn't say that, Miss Caroline."

She smiled and handed him the cup. "I would. How are things with Miss Sunglasses?"

A goofy grin spread across his face, but he didn't care. "Goin' great."

Caroline smiled. "I'm so glad. You two make such a great pair. She's a lot better for you than that Alisha ever was." She craned her neck toward the window. "Here comes Lucille. Do you know she's trying to set up my Dallas with her grand-niece?"

"She is?" Jace held back a chuckle as he realized his boss was dealing with Lucille's matchmaking skills, too.

"Poor girl. She has no idea that Lucille is trying to set up dates for her."

"Huh." Jace sipped the hot, strong coffee. "Thanks for the coffee, Miss Caroline."

"My pleasure. Next time, stop by with Sky."

"Yes, ma'am. Have a nice day." He hurried outside.

The clacks of high heels on concrete sounded before Jace could duck out of sight. He squeezed his paper disposable cup, and it crinkled. He stopped and took a deep breath.

"Jace! Jace Fisher. Wait up."

He turned around. "Hello, Miss Lucille."

She hurried over, curling her lip as she looked him over. "I sure hope you're going to wash all that off before you take out my sweet Maggie for dinner."

Anger ran through him. "I already told you, I'm *busy*."

"With what? Fixing the cottages? Visiting Claire, who doesn't remember you? Jace, we both know you don't—"

"I. Am. Seeing. Someone. She's new to town, and she's the most wonderful person I've ever met. And you know what? She doesn't care if I'm caked in dirt or not."

"Well, I—"

"Am done meddling in my life? I'm glad to hear it. I'm sure my mama would be too if she still had her senses about her."

Lucille's mouth hung open as she stared at him.

"I'd appreciate it if you'd leave me alone on this matter."

"Maggie's too classy for you, anyway. Don't expect a date with her." She huffed and stormed away.

That was the best news he'd heard all day.

TWENTY-ONE

Sky and Pixie wandered around the cottages, with Pixie stopping every two feet to sniff around or mark territory. It didn't bother Sky. She was hoping to see Jace along the way. They'd spoken the previous night for a while on the phone, and he'd told her things had finally calmed down, and he didn't have so many work emergencies. He was probably sleeping after the week he'd had.

Their date was the next night, but she wanted to see him today also—even if it was just for a few minutes.

Pixie tugged on the leash toward the beach. Sighing, Sky looked around. They'd already looped all the way around the cottages, walking by each one.

"Oh, all right. Let's go to the beach, but I need to get back and record a video or two."

They made their way to the beach and walked along the shore. Pixie jumped in and out of the water's edge. Sky paused and enjoyed the warmth. She was finally adjusting to the humidity, although she'd heard it would only get worse as the year went on.

A couple little girls came over and looked back and forth between Sky and Pixie.

"You want to pet her?"

They both nodded.

"Sure. Just be gentle. Her name's Pixie."

Both girls bent down and rubbed her fur, talking to her. The pup rolled onto her back and licked both of them, clearly enjoying the attention.

Sky's phone rang. It was Aspen. Twice in one month—what was the world coming to? She accepted the call. "Hey, Aspen."

"Sis, I have great news!"

"Oh?" Sky felt bad for hoping she wasn't going to say she'd be visiting Indigo Bay, but things were finally going well for her in the small town. She'd even started removing her sunglasses inside the shops and the cafe.

"Yeah, I'm going to be on *Murder Central, Miami* tonight. I'm playing the prime suspect. Think you can watch? It's on at nine in most places."

"I'm sure I can, but even if not, I can always record it."

Aspen squealed. "I'm so excited about this role. I can't wait to hear what you think."

"Was singing just a way to get into acting?"

"No, but I need variety in my life, you know? And acting is so much fun. I want to get more roles like this."

"A killer?"

Aspen laughed. "Not necessarily, but being a guest star for one episode. My agent was talking with the network about me playing a victim on a show with vampires. Fun, right?"

"I bet you'll have a blast."

"Time to record another commercial. Let me know what you think, 'kay? Nine tonight."

"I won't miss it," Sky promised.

"Yay. Love ya."

"You, too."

The call ended. Sky waited for the kids to run off, and then she and Pixie headed back to the cottage. Watching the show would be the perfect excuse to invite Jace back over. It felt like she hadn't even seen him all week. When they got back, a new rose bush had been planted in Pixie's favorite place to dig by the front door.

Sky cupped a flower and took in its sweet aroma. "He gave me roses."

They went inside, and she sent Jace a quick text, asking if he wanted to come over and watch the show with her. He said he did. Sky felt like she was floating on air as she went through the cottage, picking things up and figuring out what to make them to eat.

The doorbell rang at a quarter to nine. Jace stood in khaki shorts, a simple V-neck tee, and no Panthers hat. He held a bouquet of colorful tulips. Smiling, he handed them to her. "For you."

"You're so sweet! Thank you for these and the rose bush."

He beamed. "I thought you might like it."

She threw her arms around him. "I do. Come on in and have a seat. I'll put these in a vase."

A few minutes later, she and Jace were sitting on the couch, munching on freshly-made caramel cookies and bacon wrapped water chestnuts.

Jace wrapped his arm around her. "You didn't have to do all this for me."

"I wanted to. You've had one heck of a week." She kissed his cheek.

"I did, but you've more than made up for that."

Sky rubbed a red mark near his elbow. "What happened here?"

"I discovered that I'm not allergic to being stung."

"Ouch." She kissed it. "Are you okay?"

"Perfect, now."

She beamed, and then the theme music started for the show. The scene before them showed a blond businessman being strangled from behind, but didn't show the killer. A beat later, the detectives were on the scene discussing the murder.

"So, your sister did it?" Jace asked.

"She's the main suspect. That's all I know."

The TV detectives questioned everyone the blond man had worked with, and eventually discovered he had a new girlfriend—one with purple hair. That had to be

Aspen. Sure enough, after the commercial break, the detectives showed up at a huge home where Aspen, with violet-colored hair, answered. She brought them inside, where she sprawled her long legs in a short skirt across an expensive leather couch and spoke in sultry tones about her relationship with the blond businessman, who she swore wasn't serious enough to be considered a boyfriend.

At the next commercial break, Jace turned to Sky. "Aspen's really talented."

Pangs of jealousy shot through her. "To be honest, she's always been a bit of a drama queen."

"I can imagine so, as skilled an actress as she is."

Sky nodded, her voice catching in her throat.

"I'll bet she's going to get a lot more roles like this."

"You want something to drink? Wine?" Sky jumped up from the couch. She needed something to take the edge off. Why had she thought watching Aspen with Jace would be a good idea? She was just asking for him to start thinking he'd picked the wrong twin.

"Just a coke is fine."

"Sure." Sky scrambled to the kitchen, fighting the jealousy ravaging through her. Her whole life everyone had adored the dramatic and attention-seeking Aspen. After a lifetime of that, it took almost nothing for the pangs to spring to life. "He likes *you*," she whispered to herself as she grabbed some pop from the fridge. "He likes you."

"It's back on!" Jace called.

"Great." Sky poured the drinks into glasses with ice and headed back. On the screen, Aspen ran her fingers through her long, colorful hair and spoke about the businessman.

Jace laughed heartily. "She's hilarious. I never thought these shows could be funny."

Sky forced a smile. "That's Aspen for you." She handed him a glass and sat down, this time leaving some space between them. Not that Jace noticed. He leaned forward, taking in every word Aspen said.

Sighing, Sky sipped the drink, though she couldn't taste it. This was just her life—everyone enamored by Aspen, making Sky invisible. Jace laughed again at something Aspen said on screen.

He likes me. He likes me. It was so hard to fight off the old emotions. Aspen had been stealing the spotlight for as long as Sky could remember, and now even Jace was enamored by her.

Sky wanted to kick herself for thinking this could've gone any other way.

At the next break, Jace turned to her. "It's so weird. She looks just like you, but I forget you're even related because she's so different."

Sky nodded. What could she say in response? Nothing, because she was the dull, boring sister whose only screen appearances were on her blog and YouTube. "Let me refill your pop."

By the time she came back and poured the drinks, the show was back on. This time, one of Aspen's songs played in the background as it showed her sneaking around the victim's condo, appearing to tamper with potential evidence.

Jace turned to her. "Do you think she did it, or was it the jealous business partner?"

Sky had barely been able to pay attention to the storyline. "It could go either way."

"True, but I think she did it."

"Probably." She sipped the drink, knowing her annoyance was an overreaction—but that didn't make it feel any better.

At the end of the show, the detectives proved Aspen's character to be innocent.

Jace turned to Sky and smiled. "That was a lot of fun. Thanks for inviting me over."

"Sure. I missed seeing your face all week."

He cupped her chin and brushed his lips across hers. "I missed seeing you, too. Well, I better get back home. We're still on for six o'clock tomorrow, right?"

"Definitely." And the best part was that Aspen wouldn't have any part in the date.

"Good, because I told Dallas that if anything goes wrong with any of the cottages tomorrow night, he'd better be ready to roll up his sleeves and get dirty."

Sky chuckled. "I bet he loved that."

"I don't care." He gave her another quick kiss.

"Nothing's getting in the way of our date tomorrow."

She sighed as he hurried off. Was he just distracted, or did he wish she was Aspen instead of just Sky?

TWENTY-TWO

J ace knocked on his mom's door. It was only open a crack, and opened more at his knocking.

"Come in," she called.

He pushed the door and stepped inside. She sat in her rocking chair wearing the flowered bathrobe she'd had since Jace was a boy, and her hair stuck out in several directions.

It didn't appear to be one of her better days.

"Hi," Jace said.

She contorted her face as she studied him. "Do I know you?"

Jace's heart sank. She didn't even think he was Uncle Bill. He knew better than to say he was her son. That only ever upset her—not that she'd once believed him. "Yes. That's why I'm here to visit you."

"What's your name?"

"I'm Jace." He took a couple steps closer. "Does that ring a bell?"

"No, sorry. Maybe we can look through my photo

albums, and you can point yourself out. I've been looking through them all day, trying to remember who the people are."

Jace pulled one of the other seats next to her. "Let's see those."

His mom grabbed one of the albums from his elementary years. She opened to a page with pictures from a camping trip they'd taken when he was twelve.

"Who are these people?"

Jace's heart ripped in two. Would it ever get easier knowing his mom had forgotten him? He cleared his throat and pointed to his dad fishing. "That's Albert. Do you remember him?"

She shook her head. "He looks like a nice man, though. Any relation to you?"

"My dad."

"I can see the resemblance." She glanced back at the images. "One of these boys is you?"

"Yes, me and Connor. Do you remember either of us?"

"Should I?"

Jace flipped through the pages, telling her about some of his favorite family memories. She just gave him blank stares. He hated that he was the only one who remembered those good times.

Finally, he rose. "I'd better let you get some rest. I'll visit again."

"You do that. You're a nice man."

He closed the door behind him and leaned against the wall to collect himself. His chest felt tight.

A moment later, his phone rang. It was Dallas. At least a problem at one of the cottages was something he could do something about. His mom… she felt more like a lost cause than ever before. This was the first time she hadn't recognized her husband. He tended to be the one person Mom had been able to hang onto.

The phone stopped ringing before he answered. Jace would call his boss back once he was outside. On his way out, he waved to Logan, one of the regular volunteers.

Jace made his way back to the cottages, fixed something simple, and headed home to get ready for his date with Sky. He found his spirits lifting as he thought about seeing her.

He ended up ready a full half hour before needing to leave, so he paced around, trying to think of what he could do to make it even more special. They'd be taking his truck. That wasn't exactly special, but it was different—and it was sparkling clean inside and out. Jace doubted it had looked better when it was brand new.

Finally, it was time to pick her up. He went to the fridge, took the box of chocolates, and headed for the truck. It roared to life, and a minute later, he pulled into Sky's driveway. Jace grabbed the candy and practically leaped out onto the concrete.

He adjusted his collar before ringing the bell. Fancy

clothes had never been his favorite, but after going so long without wearing them, they were more uncomfortable than ever before.

When Sky opened the door, her eyes widened as she looked him over. "Wow, look at you."

He held back a smile. "I'd rather look at you." She wore a flowing, knee-length white dress full of random, colorful zig-zags. "You look beautiful. Here, these are for you."

She took the box of chocolates. "You're so sweet. Thank you." Her voice was a little flat, and her smile didn't reach her eyes. She disappeared inside and returned with a brown purse instead of the candy.

"No Pixie?" he asked.

Sky shook her head as she locked the door. "I tired her out earlier. She'll probably sleep the whole time I'm gone."

"Sounds like fun."

She nodded.

He held the passenger door for her and closed it once she was settled, then he went to his side and started it.

Sky jumped as it loudly started.

"Not used to such a noisy vehicle?" he asked.

She shook her head. "My car is so quiet you almost can't hear it."

They made small talk during the short drive, and once in the parking lot, he held her hand. She didn't thread her fingers through his like she usually did.

Inside, the three hosts all smiled at them. "Welcome to Figaro's," said a guy with a buzz cut, diamond stud in his ear, and a tie.

Jace stepped forward. "We have a reservation for two. Name's Jace Fisher."

He looked through a list and then led them through the busy restaurant to their table. As they entered the dining area, the lighting was dimmed and delicious smells intermingled, making Jace's mouth water.

"Thank you," Sky said as she scooted into the booth.

He nodded. "Javier will be your server tonight. He'll be here with water and bread shortly." He hurried back to the front of the restaurant.

Jace looked around, taking everything in. Off to the side, an enormous picture window gave them a spectacular view of the bay. Soft music played in the background. Large abstract paintings decorated the walls. Candles hung above each table, giving just enough light to read the menus.

Sky opened hers. "This place is really nice."

"It really is. I can see why everyone raves about it."

Jace glanced over his menu. The prices were astronomical, but he didn't care. It was all about the experience, and he wanted Sky to have the best possible. "Order anything you want."

"Okay. Thanks." She didn't look up.

Did she think he was bragging by telling her that? The usual excitement in her eyes had been gone since he'd arrived. Was something bothering her? Maybe something with her family?

"Is everything okay?" he asked.

Sky glanced up at him and smiled. "Yeah. This place is wonderful. I love the view." She turned back to the menu.

Jace chewed on his lower lip. Maybe she was just tired? If she said everything was okay, then it must be. He had to be imagining the awkwardness. Shrugging, he turned back to the menu, and finally settled on a filet mignon steak with a side he couldn't pronounce.

The server arrived, apologizing for the wait. He handed them lemon waters and a basket of sliced bread with a buttery dip in the middle. Sky and Jace ordered, and then dug into the appetizer. They both reached for bread and bumped their hands.

He laughed. "Sorry. You go."

She actually cracked a smile. "No, you."

Jace leaned back and shook his head. "Ladies first."

"If you insist." He finally relaxed. Maybe all the awkwardness really *had* been his imagination. They watched as a boat with a colorful sail docked not far away. Sky even scooted closer and rested her head on his shoulder. She smelled sweet and tropical, almost like pineapples. "Have you ever traveled anywhere exotic?"

Sky shook her head. "I've always wanted to go to

Hawaii or the Caribbean. Florida is the closest I've gotten."

"And you think the humidity here is bad?" Jace asked.

"I went in the winter time. It was comfortable."

"Ah, I see." His mind wandered to tropical paradises. It would be nice to take her to one someday.

Javier arrived with the food and wine. They dug in, settling into a comfortable silence. Sky finished her cut of salmon and salad before Jace even touched his side dish. She sipped her wine and gazed out at the water, looking deep in thought. He couldn't help wondering if she really was okay.

He was so out of practice on the whole dating scene, he couldn't help but feel like he was missing something. Had he gone wrong somewhere? Maybe she didn't like the chocolates? Or what if it was something else completely? He sighed, wishing he knew what was going on.

Staring at the bay, he tried to figure it out. A family walked in front of the window, distracting his thoughts. It wasn't just any family. It was Alisha, Ben, and their two kids. Jace frowned. Now the botched date was complete.

Javier came to their table. "How is everything? Can I get you anything else? Some dessert, perhaps?"

Sky rubbed her stomach. "I couldn't possibly eat more."

"Boxes, then?" He glanced at Jace's plate.

"Yes, and the check, please," Jace said. He'd lost his appetite, anyway.

"Coming right up." Javier disappeared.

Before long, Jace and Sky were back in the parking lot. He turned to her. "Would you like to take a walk along the shore? There's a really nice path leading to the boats."

"Rain check? I'm really tired."

Disappointment washed through Jace. "Sure. No problem. I'll take you home, then."

The ride back to the cottages was quiet, aside from the music playing. Once at Sky's house, she jumped out before he could open the door for her. She rushed to her front door before he could hold her hand.

He caught up with her. "Thanks for going with me. I had a really nice time."

"So did I. The restaurant was great."

She could've fooled him. "I'm glad to hear it." He leaned closer to give her a kiss, but she ducked away.

"Thank you. Goodnight."

"'Night."

She disappeared inside and closed the door. He stared at it, wondering what had gone wrong.

TWENTY-THREE

Sky woke with a headache. She rolled over, pulling the covers over her head. Pixie's barking sounded from another part of the cottage. That had to have been what woke her. Sky didn't move, hoping her pup would stop. She didn't. It was time for Pixie to go outside after being inside all night.

"Hold on!" Sky rubbed her eyes and forced herself out of bed. She stumbled around, blurry-eyed, and found the leash. Pixie jumped around her feet, yapping, until Sky snapped it onto the collar. They went out back, causing the duck family to scatter off when the door opened. Pixie chased after them, but didn't get very far due to the leash.

"Do your business." Sky yawned and squinted. The sunlight shone brightly, making her headache squeeze all the more.

Once back inside, she dug out some ibuprofen and took two. She gathered the ingredients for a smoothie, but then stopped when she realized the blender would make her head explode—or at least feel like it. Instead, she found a protein bar and ate that with fruit and a glass of almond milk.

Her gaze landed on the box of chocolates Jace had given her the night before. She sighed. That had to have been the most awkward date in the history of dates. Every time she'd looked at him, she felt like he was comparing her to Aspen. Her sister had always been the prettier twin—which made no sense given that they had the same face.

Why had she ever told him about Aspen? She could've just played dumb during the movie, saying that she could vaguely see a resemblance between her and the actress.

Then again, what if she was reading too much into Jace's praise of Aspen's acting in the murder mystery show the other night? It hadn't been like he'd been comparing the two sisters. Really, he'd only said Aspen was a good actress.

Pixie scratched on the door.

"Again?" Sky complained. Maybe a walk would do her some good. She needed to clear her head and get rid of the old insecurities—there was no reason to think Jace had been comparing her to her twin.

Pixie whined, still at the door.

"Oh, all right." Sky rose from the chair and put her dishes in the sink. "But if we're going out, I'm going to get a shower."

The pup scratched on the door again. Running water sounded outside. Probably the neighbors watering their lawn.

"You just did your business. You'll be fine." Sky rubbed Pixie's head and then got ready.

Once outside, her car caught her attention. It shone as if freshly washed. She stepped closer. Water dripped from the tire rims and a trail of suds ran down into the street. Her mouth gaped open. Had Jace washed it?

Guilt stung for doubting him. He wouldn't have done that if he didn't care. Obviously, he didn't care that Sky wasn't Aspen.

Pixie sniffed the suds and tugged on the leash. They walked down the sidewalk, but Sky's mind was far away. She needed to do something for Jace to make up for last night's date. The hurt in his eyes when she'd opted out of going for a romantic stroll had been undeniable.

It was her turn to plan something special. Maybe take him back to the other side of the bay and walk along the path like he'd wanted to do. She could put together a light meal, and they could have another picnic.

She mindlessly smiled at a few people as she walked by.

A brunette with a toddler strapped to her front stopped. "You were at Figaro's with Jace last night, weren't you?"

Sky froze. Not that she should've been surprised. It

was a town where everyone literally knew everybody else. "Yes."

"How's he doing?"

"Good. I take it you know him?"

"Very much so." The woman smiled. "I'll never forget our wedding day."

Sky fought to keep the shock off her face. Everything spun around her.

The toddler let out a cry and then screamed, kicking his mother.

"Sorry. I need to get him some food." The woman ran off.

Sky tried to move, but her feet wouldn't cooperate.

Jace had been *married*? Why hadn't he told her? Sure, Sky had said she respected his privacy, but being divorced was something he should have mentioned as soon as they admitted their feelings for each other. It wasn't a deal-breaker, but she deserved to know—and to hear it from him, not his ex-wife.

Pixie tugged on the leash.

"Let's just go back home. I need to think." They hurried back to the cottage. Everything around them was blurry and out of focus. She tripped over Pixie, barely managing to catch her balance before face-planting in the concrete.

Then she remembered her first conversation with Claire. She had mentioned Jace getting married. After she asked him about it, he'd only shown her his bare ring finger, but hadn't denied actually having gotten married.

As soon as Sky saw her shiny car, tears blurred her vision. What was she supposed to make of his mixed signals? It was too much. She hurried inside, threw herself onto the couch, and stared at a blank wall.

It made her sick that he'd been married and not bothered to tell her. How could he think that was an unimportant detail? If they were going to be in a serious relationship, she deserved to know that much.

The longer she sat there, the more infuriated she became. She wasn't going to sit there and feel sorry for herself. No, she was going to hunt down Jace Fisher and find out exactly what was going on.

Sky went into the bathroom and fixed some smudged mascara before marching to the front door.

Pixie barked at her.

"Sorry, but you have to stay home this time." She grabbed her purse and stormed outside. Hammering sounded not far away. That had to be where Jace was. Clenching her jaw, she followed the noise.

Her pulse pounded, racing through her body. Would this end everything great they had going, or would he have a reason for not telling her that made so much sense she had no other choice but to forgive him?

The hammering grew louder as she neared the pink cottage. She went around and found Jace fixing a board on the side of the house.

Sky stood there for what seemed like forever before he noticed her.

He set the hammer down and turned to her, smiling—but it faded almost immediately. "Are you okay?"

All she could do was shake her head.

"What's wrong?"

She took a deep breath. It still felt like the world was spinning around her. "I know I told you that I respect your right to privacy, but I do deserve to know anything major about you. That's only fair."

Jace nodded. "I understand, but what has you so upset? Do you need to sit down? Are you thirsty?" He reached for a water bottle.

"No!" she snapped.

He studied her. "What do you need, then?"

Was he really that dense? She wanted to shake him. "For you to tell me anything about you that I should know if we're going to keep seeing each other!"

TWENTY-FOUR

Jace stared at Sky, struck with confusion. "I can't think of anything."

"Seriously?" she yelled.

He'd never seen her so upset. "Maybe we should go somewhere a little more private to talk. There are people inside the cottage. Honeymooners."

Sky's face contorted, and if he didn't know better, he'd have thought he'd seen steam shoot out her ears. "Let me guess. You don't want them to hear what you have to tell me?"

"No. It's not that." He made sure to keep his voice low and steady. "I just don't want to bother them. Do you want to go to the beach? Or to your place?"

"No! I just want you to tell me the truth."

Jace felt like he'd been punched in the gut. "I assure you I've never lied to you."

"Well, you've gone out of your way to hide at least one major thing from me." Her eyes narrowed and her mouth formed a straight line.

"I'll be right back," he called to the couple inside. He reached for Sky, but she yanked her arm away and glowered at him. His heart thundered against his ribcage. "Follow me."

"Fine."

Jace led her to a quiet part of the beach, taking advantage of the silence to try and figure out what the heck was going on. Things had been a little awkward at the restaurant, but now she was taking it to a whole new level. It was starting to irritate him. He stopped at a bench underneath some trees. He gestured for her to sit.

Sky folded her arms and shook her head.

"Would you tell me what's going on?" he demanded. "If you're going to accuse me of something, at least tell me what you think I did."

"What I *think* you did?" she exclaimed.

He took a deep breath. "Tell me what I did, would you?"

She stared at him, her face growing redder by the moment. "I just want you to tell me anything major in your life that I, as someone dating you, should know about. That's all I ask."

"That's fair." His mind went over anything important he may have left out. "You know about my mom."

Sky nodded but her expression didn't relax any.

"My dad and brother both died."

"Anything else? Something big you might be leaving

out?"

"Do you want me to list out for you every heartache I've ever experienced? Because that could take a while." He glared back at her, his irritation growing by the moment. "Do you want every detail about how my dad and brother died? Is that it? Maybe talk about my grandpa's last days as cancer destroyed him?"

Her expression softened. "No, of course not. I said something big that *you* did." She stared him down again.

Jace's irritation flipped to anger. "It sounds like you already know something. Why don't you tell me so I can explain it?"

"Because I want to hear it from you!"

He clenched his fists, wanting to punch one of the trees. "How, pray tell, am I supposed to do that if I don't even know what you're talking about?"

"Something *major*. A detail that you wouldn't want to leave out from someone you care about."

Jace counted to ten, then twenty. "If you know, just tell me."

"Like I said, I want to hear it from you."

The argument was going nowhere, and there was no way he could figure out what she wanted to know. It wasn't like he'd been to jail or anything serious like that. His life, apart from the many heartaches, had been pretty dull.

She tapped her foot.

He snapped his attention toward her. "I'm sick of playing games. Either tell me what you know, or don't."

Her eyebrows came together, but she said nothing.

Jace took a deep breath. "You know, if I didn't care, I'd just walk away. But I do care—I just don't know what you want me to tell you."

"How can you not know?" she demanded.

"Because you won't tell me!"

They stared each other down, neither saying anything.

Sky put her hands on her hips. "You still won't tell me?"

"I can't, since I don't know what it is." He narrowed his eyes.

"This is ridiculous."

"You're telling me." He clenched his jaw so tightly he expected to feel teeth cracking.

"I'm done dealing with this garbage."

Jace snorted. "Seriously?"

"Just tell me!"

"I don't know what you want to know!"

"Oh! You're infuriating."

He gave her a double-take. "You're the one playing mind games."

"Mind games?" she exclaimed.

"You won't tell me what you know!"

"I don't have to put up with this. If you don't want to tell me, fine. If you change your mind, you know where to find me." She stared at him, obviously still expecting him to read her mind.

"Great." He crossed his arms over his chest. His mind raced with things he wanted to say but would regret later, so he kept quiet.

They stared each other down. Then Jace's phone rang. It was Dallas.

"I have to go. I'm supposed to be working."

"Well, I guess we'll have to finish this conversation later."

He nodded. That was probably for the best, given how angry he was at that moment. He would feel a lot better after physical labor.

TWENTY-FIVE

S ky stopped typing again. Tears kept blurring her vision, making it impossible to see the screen. She blinked them away and tried to focus on the words. They all ran together, making no sense.

"Great. Now I'm too upset to keep up with my blog." She got up and walked through the cottage, trying to clear her head, but it was useless. The only thing that would help would be if Jace told her about being married—and that was never going to happen because he had no intention of ever telling her. She'd given him a chance, and he'd told her she was playing games with him!

It'd been two days, and Sky didn't feel any better than she had when they'd argued. She'd eaten enough chocolate and ice cream to gain four pounds.

The doorbell rang. Probably the makeup samples she was expecting. If she could pull herself together, she might be able to record an unboxing and a makeup tutorial. Her readers were bugging her for another post.

Pixie ran around in front of the door, barking.

"Okay, okay." She went to the door and opened it.

It wasn't a package.

"Haley?" she exclaimed.

Sky's long-time friend from back home threw her arms around her, squeezing her. "It looks like I got here just in time."

"What…? How…?" Sky shook her head. "I told you not to bother coming down."

"And you thought I'd listen?" Haley arched a brow and wiped some blonde hair behind her ears. "Mind if I come inside? The humidity's killing me."

Sky stepped aside, letting her in. "Why'd you come? You're in the middle of planning your wedding."

"Because you're more important. I brought wine and chocolate." Haley grinned as she shrugged her bags to the floor. "There's no way I could let you suffer alone."

"Seriously, your wedding."

"My future sister-in-law is a wedding planner for celebrities, remember? Dakota has it covered. If she has any questions, she'll call me. But she won't, because she understands the importance of girl time."

Sky embraced her friend. "You don't know how much this means to me."

"Are you kidding?" Haley pulled out an enormous bottle of wine. "Where's your corkscrew?"

"Over here." Sky found it, and Haley took it from

her.

"Sit at the table while I get everything ready."

"But I—"

"Sit. Now."

Sky did as she was told and watched as Haley set up the kitchen table with tubs of ice cream, wine glasses, tissues, some DVDs, and several boxes of chocolate— like Sky really needed more, but she wasn't going to turn it down.

Haley finally sat, and she handed Sky an empty bowl and spoon along with ice cream toppings. "Now tell me all about it, starting with how you met this Jace character."

Sky scooped several flavors of ice cream into her bowl as she told Haley the whole story. By the time she finished telling her friend about the fight on the beach, they'd gone through two bowls, plus half a box of chocolates and a glass of wine. Sky broke down, sobbing.

Haley handed her a tissue. "Let's take this to the couch." She handed Sky the box of tissues, then she gathered the DVDs and wine, putting them on the coffee table.

Sky sobbed so hard her breathing became labored. Haley handed her more tissues and then put her arm around Sky. "Let it all out."

"I should've known better—I really should have. What made me think I could have a relationship that actually worked?"

"Because you're worth it. We just need to find a guy who recognizes that."

Sky frowned. "I thought Jace was that guy."

Haley tilted her head. "Do you still?"

Sky couldn't answer. She *wanted* him to be, but was he?

"You don't think there's any chance there's a miscommunication?" Haley patted Sky's hand.

"I don't see how." Sky thought back over their interactions. He'd always been mannerly and honorable. All of this was so out of character for him. Why would he keep his marriage a secret? Especially since it was obviously in the past.

"What did he say when you confronted him about being married?" Haley asked.

Sky paused. She hadn't actually told him what was bothering her. But then again, he should've known.

"Well, the good news is that you can move anywhere that has wifi. That's all you need for work, right?" Haley smiled.

"Yeah."

"Do you want to come back to Enchantment Bay?"

Sky sighed, feeling deflated. "I just paid for another month here."

"Can't you get a refund for the time unused?"

"I don't think so."

"You don't have to worry about that now, anyway.

Here, pick a movie. I made sure not to pick anything Aspen was in."

Sky cracked a smile and then looked through the stack, finally settling on *Someone Like You*. Before long, Sky found herself laughing at the hilariousness of it. They ended up going through the entire stack, and Sky dozed off halfway through *Jerry Maguire.*

She woke to the aromas of bacon and coffee. Sky threw off the blanket and sat up, a headache making her dizzy. "What are you doing?"

Haley grinned at her. "Making breakfast. What does it look like?"

Sky's stomach rumbled. Coffee and food would probably help. "Thanks."

"No problem. Come on over here and eat up. We have a busy day ahead of us."

"We do?"

"You're showing me around town and then we're going to the beach."

"I hope that doesn't involve wearing a swimsuit. I think I've gained ten pounds since yesterday."

Haley flipped over a hash brown. "Could've fooled me. Besides, even if you did, a walk around this humid town will burn all that right off you. Come on—time to eat."

Sky rubbed her eyes and stumbled her way to the table. "Thanks for all this. I really didn't expect you to fly in."

"What are friends for? Besides, my aunt works for the airline. It didn't cost me more than the rental car and the snacks I picked up."

"Still…"

Haley set a full plate of scrambled eggs, bacon, hash browns, and toast in front of her. Then she brought over a cup of coffee and some creamer before sitting with her own food. "Do you feel any better?"

"Other than this headache, I think so."

"Food will help." Haley poured ketchup onto her hash browns.

Sky dug into her eggs. Things actually did seem a little better than they had been the night before. The heartache still lingered, of course, but there seemed to be a light at the end of the tunnel.

TWENTY-SIX

Jace pulled his sketch pad out and tried to get comfortable on the sand. His new secret place left a lot to be desired. If only Sky hadn't found the one he'd relied on for years. But she had, and he would have to make do with this new hiding spot.

He craned his neck to get a better view of the water. If he sat like that for an hour, he'd end up with a sore neck. Sighing, he readjusted himself. It didn't help much.

If there wasn't a chance Sky would find him at the other place, he would've gone there. Not after the things she had said. He'd just deal with not having as good of a view.

Why had he allowed himself to think a relationship could work? Because he'd let himself become smitten by the pretty traveler—but that wasn't a mistake he was going to make again. He was done with women. He couldn't figure them out, nor did he want to. It was too much trouble, and one thing he didn't need in his life was more heartache. He should've known better. Keeping everyone away was his best course of action. He hadn't gotten hurt the whole time he kept everyone at an arm's length. The second he let someone in? Pain.

A rumbling sounded in the distance. Jace sat taller and stared out over the water. There were dark clouds a little ways away. He checked the weather app on his phone. It called for the possibility of a brief thunderstorm. He put the phone back and studied the skyline. A tiny flash of light appeared in the midst of the menacing clouds.

"Looks like I found something interesting to draw." Jace grabbed a dark pencil and started near the top of the page. The edge of the sky was growing darker by the moment. Another flash of lightning. More rumbling.

He drew furiously, trying to keep up with the moving storm. The skyline intrigued him—it was still sunny and beautiful over Indigo Bay, but farther away, the bright blue melted into the black thunderclouds. The storm was so far away, nobody playing by the water seemed to notice. It was headed their way, so it was only a matter of time.

Jace went through half a dozen sheets of paper, drawing the scenery as the storm moved their way. A chilly wind picked up and the sky over Indigo Bay turned gray. Some of the beachgoers gathered their things and ran off. Others watched, curious, while some people still hadn't noticed anything unusual—they just kept jogging, building sandcastles, swimming, and sunbathing. It was quite a sight, and Jace's hand cramped as he drew the scene before him.

Thunder rumbled, this time closer and louder. Nobody missed that. The beach cleared quickly, leaving only Jace and a few others. He was mesmerized by the array of colors from the clouds and the way they reflected onto the bay. He had to sharpen some of his pencils several times.

The wind picked up and started to blow his bag. Jace grabbed it just in time and pulled it over his shoulder. There wouldn't be much time before he would have to leave the beach. A twig blew his way. He ducked, barely missing it as it flew over his head.

It was time to leave. He stuck his sketchpad and pencil in his bag and ran home. A few drops of rain splashed down, but it was a far cry from the impending downpour.

Just as he opened his front door, a loud crack of thunder shook the ground. Jace's ears rang as he entered the empty house and slammed the door. He sat on the sofa and watched the storm through a window as it came in. His eyelids grew heavy, and he watched as long as he could keep them open.

His dreams were filled with Sky's beautiful smile, and when he woke, his heart was as heavy as it had been with all the other heartbreaks he'd suffered. It felt like he was standing at the altar alone again, only this time, he didn't have hundreds of eyes staring at him.

Jace got up, grabbed his bag, and sat by the sliding glass door. The clouds had gotten a lot darker. He checked the time. His nap had only been an hour—it was barely past noon—but it looked like late evening outside. Everything lit up for a moment, followed immediately by a clap of loud thunder. His walls shook.

It was time to relax and be glad he was inside. Once the storm passed, he would be busy with the cottages. These storms tended to pull boards loose and cause leaks or even flooding. He made himself a cup of coffee and sat at the table, flipping through his sketch book starting at his most recent drawing. The storm had progressed a lot since he'd been on the beach.

Once he was done, he would draw the scene before him. It only seemed fitting considering how many pictures he'd drawn of the storm slowly making its way to Indigo Bay. He continued looking at the drawings of the beach and various wildlife until he came to one he'd sketched of Sky—he hadn't even realized it when he'd drawn it. He'd been in the zone, and completely entranced by the storm.

Jace froze, his breath hitched. He'd captured her well—her stunning eyes, captivating smile, and sweet spirit. Well, sweet until she started accusing him of who-knows-what since she wouldn't even tell him what it was she thought she knew. He gazed at the picture, longing for what they'd had. It had been magical and far too short-lived.

It was for the best that it ended, though. If it had gone on for a long time, the hurt of breaking up would be all that much worse. It was already bad enough.

He went back to the blank pages and drew what he could see outside. The storm already seemed to be losing steam. He hadn't seen any new lightning. A branch tapped against the cottage, reminding him that the wind hadn't lightened up any yet.

Time escaped him as he put the pencil to the paper again. Jace drew several more pictures of the storm. He was in the zone, almost feeling like the sketches were drawing themselves. That was when he did his best work.

When he was done, he set down his pencil and glanced at the image before him. He jumped in surprise. It was Sky. He'd drawn her face without even realizing it. His heart leaped into his throat.

Jace closed the pad and stuffed it back into the bag. He needed some air.

TWENTY-SEVEN

Sky stretched. "Do you want to watch another movie?"

Haley glanced out the window. "It looks like the storm has died down. Why don't you show me around town?"

"It's still windy. Pixie could blow away."

Haley didn't laugh. "That might've been a possibility earlier, but not now. Come on. We need to get out of the house."

And risk running into Jace? Sky shook her head and flipped through the streaming choices. "Hey, look. This is new. It's about a clothing designer who goes crazy and kills everyone that—"

"I saw it in the theater. Get your coat."

Sky arched an eyebrow. "You do realize it's still going to be hot outside, don't you? The humidity's probably going to be worse than before."

Haley groaned. "You're right. This isn't a northwestern storm."

"I bet a movie isn't sounding so bad now, is it? We can find something else to watch. What about that new mini-series based on that Stephen King novel?"

"We need to get you out of the house. I want to see that cafe you told me about."

"It's just a cafe—they serve coffee, sweet tea, and snacks."

Haley gave her a knowing look. "What's it going to take to get you outside?"

"Can you guarantee I won't run into Jace?"

"So that's what this is about. Why don't you show me his picture, and I'll keep an eye out for you?"

Sky glared at her. "You're impossible."

"What are friends for? Show me his picture. I'll protect you."

Sighing, Sky pulled out her phone. Haley wouldn't give up, so she needed to accept the fact they were going to walk around Indigo Bay in the wind and puddles. She found a selfie they'd taken on the beach.

Haley snatched the phone. "Oh, he's gorgeous—I mean, he looks horrible. Mean and rude. Just plain rotten."

"You're not convincing at all." Sky frowned.

"I've never been a good liar. Come *on*. We're leaving, and the longer you stall, the longer we're staying out."

"Fine." Begrudgingly, Sky picked up Pixie's leash. "Wanna go for a walk?" Her voice was so flat, the pup didn't even notice she was talking to her. Pixie just stayed at her spot by the sliding door, watching what remained of the storm.

Haley patted her legs. "Pixie! Wanna go for a walk?"

She spun around and barked, running over to Sky, who attached the leash.

"That's how it's done," Haley teased.

"Let's just get this over with." Sky found Pixie's mauve raincoat and tiny, matching boots.

"Those are the cutest things I've ever seen," Haley gushed. "Does she actually wear them?"

"We'll find out. She kept them on long enough for me to get pictures for my blog last week." Sky held Pixie in her lap while she slid on the outfit. Pixie jumped up and ran around as soon as she was dressed.

Haley pulled out her phone and snapped a couple pictures. Sky pulled the hood over Pixie's head, and they all made their way outside. The wind wasn't as bad as Sky had thought, and the rain had nearly stopped.

"Ugh, you were right about the humidity." Haley pulled her shirt out and fanned it.

Sky had to admit it was pretty bad. "It still beats the way the cold clings to us back home."

They debated about which place was better to be caught in a storm until they had nearly reached Sweet Caroline's.

Haley stopped. "Don't look now."

Sky's stomach twisted in knots. "Jace?"

"Worse."

"What could be…?" Sky's voice trailed off.

A group of teenage girls in red and white cheer uniforms streaming out from a yellow school bus with *Cheer Camp* scrawled on the side. The girls were headed toward the cafe, and the ones nearest were whispering and pointing at Sky.

She took a step back. "I'm leaving."

It was too late. The girls were running toward them, and they were blocking the way back to the cottages.

Sky's stomach lurched. She picked up Pixie and prepared to run. Her legs wouldn't cooperate.

"Aspen!" one girl called out, waving her hands.

"I can't believe she's here," said another.

"In this little, boring town of all places."

Before Sky knew it, girls crowded all around her, talking over each other. They begged for autographs and selfies with her. Sky struggled to breathe. Dizziness overcame her. "I need space."

None of them heard her. They only crowded around her all the more, pushing against her. Why hadn't she brought her sunglasses? She should've known better. But with the dark weather, she'd had a momentary lapse in judgment.

Lights flashed all around her as people snapped pictures with their phones. Someone squeezed her arm. Sky yanked out of the grasp, but then noticed it was Haley.

They pushed their way out of the crowd of cheerleaders, barely squeezing out. Once they did, Sky ran around them, tears blurring her vision.

"Aspen!"

"Wait!"

"Come back here!"

Pixie squirmed to get out of Sky's arms. She held on tighter, afraid for her pup's safety. Finally, they made it back to the cottage. Huffing and puffing, Sky dug the keys out of her purse.

Haley caught up. She glanced back. "That was crazy."

"Welcome to my world." Sky unlocked the door and rushed inside.

"I've seen people ask you for autographs, but that took it to a whole new level."

Sky slammed the door shut and locked the deadbolt. "That was definitely the worst—and I never would've guessed that it could actually be crazier here in Indigo Bay than it was in Seattle."

"Maybe they're more used to seeing celebrities there?" Haley asked.

"All I know is that I'm done with this place." Sky marched into the bedroom, pulled out her suitcase, and grabbed clothes from her closet.

"Don't you want to sleep on this? I thought you liked it here."

Tears blurred Sky's vision. "There's nothing here for me. At least if I go back to Enchantment Bay, you'll be there. Plus, I won't have reminders of Jace."

Haley frowned. "Are you sure that's what you want?"

Sky blinked the tears away and nodded. "I don't even care if I lose a whole month's rent. I'm out of here."

"I'll help you pack." Haley picked up another suit-case.

TWENTY-EIGHT

The warm wind whipped droplets of rain against Jace. He ignored it and wandered mindlessly through the cottages, checking for damage, but mostly trying to clear his head. A large branch had scraped against the red cottage, but luckily hadn't caused any structural harm. Some boards had pulled loose from the purple cottage. A small tree had taken out the deck on the dark green cottage—that would take some time to fix. Other than that, everything seemed to have survived the storm without much excitement.

He still had to check the dark blue cottage. His stomach twisted in knots. He wanted to know if Sky was okay, but he wanted to avoid actually seeing her.

Jace headed for her place but had every intention of turning around if he happened to see her. He just wanted to know that she was okay and what, if any, damage the cottage had taken. That was all.

When the home came into view, the first thing he noticed was something piled up next to Sky's car. He kept his focus on that as he neared. After his vision focused, he realized it was luggage.

He froze mid-step.

Was she leaving? As in, moving away?

Sky stepped outside and added two more suitcases to the pile before returning inside.

Terror gripped him. She couldn't leave Indigo Bay. More specifically, Sky couldn't leave *him*.

Jace had to do something. But what? Could anything he said make a difference?

She came back outside, added another large bag, and promptly went back in.

His breath hitched. They needed to talk about whatever their fight had been about—as in really talk. She needed to tell him what was going on, and he needed to open himself up to her completely. He had to risk it, even if she still decided to leave. If it took four hours to tell his life story and go over every painful detail to keep her in town, he would do it. He'd even tell her the humiliating story of being left at the altar, scorned by his fiancée and so-called best friend.

Jace rushed over to the pile of luggage and grabbed the two largest pieces and lugged them inside.

Sky came over from the hall with another suitcase in hand, and her eyes widened when she saw him. "What are you doing?"

"Bringing your stuff back inside."

"I can see that, but why?"

His heart pounded like a jackhammer. "I can't let you leave."

"You… you're not *letting* me leave?"

"We need to talk."

Her eyes narrowed. "There's nothing to talk about. You made that abundantly clear before."

Jace took a deep breath and considered his words. He didn't want to say anything that would further upset her. "I'm not sure what it is that you want me to tell you, but I'll tell you anything—anything at all. No matter how painful or humiliating."

She studied him. "You had your chance. It's clear you're more interested in keeping major details secret." She made a beeline for the door.

He stepped in front of it.

"Excuse me. I need to get by."

Jace shook his head. "We need to talk. I'll tell you everything."

"Everything?" She raised an eyebrow.

"Yes. I'll tell you every painful detail of my life if that's what it takes." His voice cracked. "And you can walk away when I'm done if that's what you think is best. I won't stop you."

She paused. "Then tell me the big thing you've been keeping from me. Start there." Sky stared him down, but her eyes misted.

Seeing her in pain was all it took to break him. He wrapped his arms around her and pulled her close. "I'll tell you anything you want to know."

Sky tried to pull away but then stopped. She didn't put her arms around him, but she leaned against him as he rubbed her back.

Jace sighed in relief. At least he had her attention—he now stood a chance of convincing her to stay. He tried to figure out where to begin, and she pulled away.

"We should bring your luggage inside first." That would buy him a few minutes to figure out what to say.

She shook her head. "I want to hear it from you before I make a decision."

"This could take a while. Someone could steal your stuff."

"In Indigo Bay?" She arched a brow.

"It could happen."

"Just tell me what I want to know, then I'll know you're serious."

His stomach tightened. "Of course I'm serious! I'm here, aren't I? And since I don't know what it is that you want me to tell you, it could take a while to get there."

She stared at him, her expression conflicted.

"Or you could tell me what you want to know. That could speed up the process quite a bit."

"Why won't you tell me?" she exclaimed.

Jace threw his head back. "What do you want to know?"

The front door creaked, and in walked a blonde Jace had never seen. Her eyes widened. "I'll come back."

Sky grabbed onto her. "No. Stay."

Jace tilted his head and gave the stranger a curious glance. "Who are you?"

"She's helping me move." Sky stepped closer to the lady. "You want to talk, talk."

"I meant in private." Did she honestly expect him to pour his heart out in front of someone he didn't know?

Tears shone in Sky's eyes. "Whatever you have to say, you can say in front of Haley."

Haley put a hand up. "Really, I can go. I *should*, Sky."

Sky glanced back and forth between the two of them. A single tear slipped from her eye as her gaze locked with Jace's.

He stepped forward, wiped the tear with his thumb, and kissed her soft, sweet lips. She tasted like white wine and milk chocolate. Sky stiffened, and then relaxed, putting a hand on his arm.

TWENTY-NINE

Sky clung to Jace and kissed him back, a wild range of emotions welling up inside her. He smelled like sandalwood, and his touch was both comforting and electrifying at the same time.

Jace pulled back, ending the kiss almost as suddenly as it had begun. His eyes were dazed, as she was sure hers were too. Sky gasped for air, desperate for a coherent thought. She couldn't think straight in his arms.

Sky cleared her throat and took a step back. "We'd better get going, Haley."

Disappointment washed over Jace's expression. "You're leaving now?"

A lump formed in Sky's throat. "I need to."

"You won't hear me out?" His eyes pleaded with her.

It was almost enough to get her to stay. She couldn't do it. Everything in Indigo Bay was part of her past now. She stepped over to the coffee table and grabbed her keys.

"Sky, wait."

More tears threatened. She needed to get out before she caved. "Excuse me."

He didn't move, so she pushed past him before she changed her mind. Jace ran outside and stood behind her car.

"What are you doing?" she exclaimed.

"If you leave, you're going to have to run me over first."

She gave him a double-take. "You're crazy."

"For you."

Sky blinked back the threatening tears. "Don't do this."

"You leave me no other choice."

Haley came outside. "I, uh, I'm going to put the suitcases in the car."

"No," Sky said, not taking her gaze from Jace. "Not yet."

"Really?" Jace asked.

"The rain's picking up," Haley said. "Everything's going to get soaked."

Sky swallowed, trying to push down the lump in her throat. "Then I'll bring it back in—for now."

Jace shook his head. "No, you won't. I will."

She stared at him, unable to find words.

He brushed his lips across hers, grabbed some suitcases, and hurried inside.

Haley turned to her. "I'll head over to that cafe and

let you guys talk. The poor guy turned pale as a ghost when you told him to talk in front of me."

"Please stay. I don't think I can do this without you."

"You can. Did you see the look on his face? He really cares about you—a lot. I have a feeling you're going to stay here after this."

Sky frowned. "Don't be so sure." She grabbed a suitcase and headed inside. Haley followed her, and as they came in, Jace went back out. He returned with nearly half the luggage. He had suitcases stuffed under his arms and held two in each hand. "Where do you want these?"

"Anywhere," Sky said. "Don't hurt yourself."

He snickered. "I won't."

Haley and Sky went out into the rain with him and brought the rest inside.

"Well, I'll leave you two alone." Haley brushed some rain from her shirt.

Sky shook her head. "I already told you no. We can go for a walk."

"You don't mind the rain?" Jace asked.

"I'm from the northwest. It helps me to feel at home."

"Perfect." He held her hand, threading his fingers between hers. "Where's Pixie?"

"Sleeping in her bed in one of the spare rooms. I didn't want her getting out while we packed the car."

"It isn't the same without her running around."

Haley threw Sky an approving glance. "Want me to grab Pixie?"

"Yes," Jace said. "She'd enjoy the walk."

Sky's heart warmed, feeling like it was growing in size.

Jace squeezed her hand.

Haley returned with Pixie, and handed the leash to Jace. "Have fun, you three."

Sky let go of Jace's hand and embraced her friend. "Thank you."

She squeezed her back. "Just go make up. I don't want to see you again until you can introduce me to your boyfriend."

"We'll see." Her doubt was fading, and as long as Jace could be truthful about his marriage, she would most likely be willing to stay. It was probably really painful for him since he was being so secretive about it. She turned back to Jace, who was patting Pixie and speaking to her in a high-pitched voice. She beamed, watching him with her pup.

Jace turned to her and rose. "Ready?"

She gave a little nod and laced her fingers through his. Haley gave her a thumbs-up as they left through the sliding glass door. They walked in silence, stepping over branches and other debris from the storm.

After they reached the beach, he turned to her. "Should we go to our spot?"

Her heart warmed at him calling it theirs. "Okay."

When they got there, Jace cleared some leaves and branches, and they snuggled together on the root-chair. He put his arm around her, and she leaned against him, feeling at home. Pixie jumped up and made herself comfortable, half on his lap and half on Sky's.

Jace cleared his throat. "Do you want me to start at the beginning, or would you like to tell me what has your feathers so ruffled?"

Her heart raced. She blurted out, "Why didn't you tell me you were married?"

"What?" He sounded confused.

"I ran into your ex-wife the other day."

"My *ex-wife*?" Now he sounded angry. "Is that what Alisha told you?"

Sky thought back to the conversation. "I believe her exact words were, 'I'll never forget the day of our wedding.'"

"That's because that's all it was. Our wedding day. We never got married, though."

"What? What do you mean?"

Jace's face tensed. "She never showed up. Left me standing at the altar, looking like a fool in front of everyone we knew. She and my best friend left town together that day."

Sky's mouth dropped. "I-I had no idea."

He laughed bitterly. "I'll bet she left that out."

"Yeah." They sat in silence as Sky took in what he

said. "What happened?"

"Apparently, I grew too boring for her after my father and brother died, and then my mother forgot me. Neither of them even had the decency to tell me ahead of time. I had to find out at the altar in front of everyone I knew."

"I'm so sorry."

Jace shrugged. "Probably for the best. At least I saw her true colors before making the biggest mistake of my life."

Sky took a deep breath. "I can't imagine how much that must've hurt. Jace, I'm really sorry I didn't ask you about it before jumping to conclusions."

"I'm sure Alisha told you a pretty convincing story."

"Still, I should've asked for your side before accusing you like that."

"We all fly off the handle from time to time."

She leaned her head against him. "It's no excuse."

"I'm just glad you decided to hear me out."

"So, you must've had a really hard time when all that stuff happened with your family."

He let out a long, slow breath. "I always knew I'd have less time with my parents since it took them more than twenty years to have Connor and me. Didn't make it any easier when Dad passed away from kidney failure, though. Then before any of us had a chance to recover from that, Connor was struck by a falling beam at his construction site. Died immediately with no pain—

that's supposed to make me feel better, but it doesn't. My brother's gone, and he's never coming back." He wiped his eyes and sucked in a deep breath.

"I can't even imagine."

Jace looked at her, his eyes red. Tears fell when he blinked. It tore her up seeing him so hurt. "It sent Mom over the edge. Now she lives somewhere between the past and an imaginary world. Then when I thought things couldn't get worse, the only girl I ever dated left me at the altar, taking my lifelong best friend with her."

Sky felt so stupid for getting worked up over being mistaken for her famous twin. He probably thought she was horribly petty.

"So then I buried myself in my work and art, leaving no time for anyone else. Until you showed up."

The lump in her throat from earlier returned. She knew if she said anything, she'd be in tears too.

He held her gaze. "I don't know how I'm supposed to deal with all of it."

Sky's heart broke in two. She pulled him against her, pulled off his hat, and ran her hands through his hair. "You're supposed to cry and scream about how unfair it is, and after that, talk about it with someone who cares. Then repeat the whole miserable process over and over again until it starts to hurt a little less." He shook in her arms. Sky heard his muffled sobs. She kissed the top of his head. "That's it—let it all out."

She rubbed his back as he continued shaking, and

his tears wet the collar of her shirt. She teared up thinking of all he'd gone through—and alone, no less!

After a while, Jace sat back and wiped his tears away. The skin around his eyes was red and splotchy. "I've never cried like that. Not since I was a kid, anyway."

"You've never mourned at all?"

He shrugged. "I took my frustrations out with a hammer on the cottages."

"That's not grieving."

"I'm starting to see that."

She squeezed his hand. "Do you feel any better?"

"Actually, I do. A little bit. That's offset by my embarrassment, though, at this pathetic display of weakness. I'm sorry. I shouldn't have dumped this on you. I should have dealt with this years ago, on my own."

"Are you kidding me? I'm happy to be dumped on. And by the way, you're the strongest person I know." Sky leaned over and brushed her lips across his. "I'll have to stay in town so you can do that over and over again. It's all part of the process, and like I said, you need someone who cares to listen."

He pulled her close and kissed her passionately. "I think I love you."

She grinned. "I think I love you, too."

THIRTY

J ace clung to the leash as they neared the edge of the beach. "She's surprisingly strong."

"Tiny, but mighty." Sky laughed. "That's my Pixie."

Good heavens, Sky was breathtaking. He grinned at her and then stepped around a branch. "You know, I might just have to convince Dallas to hire someone to help me with this cleanup."

"I can help you."

"Well, I was actually thinking of someone a little more permanent."

"Oh?" Sky asked, tilting her head curiously. "Why's that?"

"I think I'm done being the only handyman for the cottages. It's really a two-person job, and now that I found someone worth spending my time with—"

Sky kissed him. "You're totally amazing, you know that?"

"I wouldn't say that."

"Of course you wouldn't. That's what makes you so

wonderful." She toyed with his hair and held his gaze.

Jace's breath caught. He was still feeling raw from having broken down in her arms, but it had been refreshing at the same time. He'd never given into his emotions like that, but she'd been right. It had helped. And even better yet, she continued giving him adoring glances—she didn't think poorly of him for having a hard time with things or having been left at the altar.

Sky took his hand again, and they made their way to the cottage with Pixie tugging on the leash and barking. Before they reached the door, she turned to him and stared into his eyes. "Anytime you need to talk, or even sit in silence and just not be alone, let me know. Okay?"

He nodded.

"I'm serious, Jace. If it's midnight or three in the morning or I'm in the middle of making a video, I'll drop everything and be there."

Jace tried to speak, but the words wouldn't come. His already exposed emotions were threatening to rise to the surface again. He cleared his throat. "Thanks."

She squeezed his hand. "As long as you know I'm serious. It's hard enough dealing with one loss, I can't imagine dealing with four major hits."

"What did I do to deserve you?"

Sky traced his jawline and gazed into his eyes. "I'm just glad my friend told me about Indigo Bay."

"We should definitely send her a thank you card."

"That's not a bad idea. But speaking of friends, we

should get inside. Poor Haley must be bored out of her mind."

Jace gave her a quick kiss and they headed for the cottages, but before they made it past the beach, Sky froze.

"What's the matter?" he asked.

"Nothing. Let's go."

He looked around. Ben and Alisha were headed their way, laughing and holding hands.

Sky tugged on his arm. "Come on. Haley's waiting for us."

Jace shook his head. "No. I need to talk to them. This town is too small to have to worry about avoiding anyone."

Her beautiful eyes widened. "Are you sure?"

He nodded, threaded his fingers through hers, and walked straight toward Alisha and Ben. They hadn't noticed Sky and Jace yet. He marched toward them until they stood directly in front of the other couple.

They stopped, both giving Jace a questioning look.

Ben put an arm around Alisha. "Excuse us."

Jace stood taller and shook his head. "No. We need to talk."

"Now?" Alisha exclaimed.

"Yes. This town isn't big enough for the four of us *and* your attitudes. I don't ever expect us to sit around playing cards, but we can at least be civil."

Alisha and Ben exchanged a glance.

"I'm serious," Jace said. "If you have anything you want to say to either one of us, say it now."

"What's your problem?" Ben asked.

Jace clenched his jaw. "You've both been rude ever since you got here. And Alisha, you need to apologize for telling my girlfriend that you and I were ever married."

"You what?" Ben exclaimed.

Her mouth dropped open. "I swear, I never said that."

Sky gasped.

"Well, I may have *implied* it."

Ben's nostrils flared and he looked at Sky. "Alisha never married Jace."

Jace stared Alisha down. "You ready to apologize?"

"Fine. I'm sorry I gave you the impression that I was anything other than his fiancée. I won't bother either one of you guys again." She looked at Jace. "How was that?"

"Great, if you meant it."

Alisha grabbed Ben's hand. "Come on."

Ben didn't budge. "I can't believe you told her that."

"It was nothing personal." Alisha pulled on him.

"How could it not be? *We're* married…" Ben's voice trailed off as they walked away.

Sky turned to Jace and kissed his cheek. "They seem perfect for each other."

He returned the kiss. "She did me a favor, and now

I have someone so much better."

She beamed and then they headed for the cottages, holding hands. Jace scratched his knee and realized sand had gotten into his pants.

"You mind if we stop by my place first?" He continued shaking his leg, trying to get more sand out. "I need to change. Sand is out this season."

She burst out laughing. "You're so funny, and no, I don't mind stopping. Take all the time you need. I've never seen your place."

His mind raced, hoping it was clean. He wasn't one to leave underwear lying around, but it would be just his luck to have when she came over.

Once inside—it was clean—he invited her to sit on the couch while he changed. When he came out, wearing fresh clothes, Sky held a pad of paper.

His artwork. Nobody had ever seen that. He opened his mouth, but no words would come.

She glanced up at him, holding a sketch of herself. "This is really good."

At least she hadn't noticed the horror ripping through him.

"Why didn't you tell me you're an artist?"

Jace found his voice. "I'm not. It's just stress relief."

"You really should display these. Actually, you could sell these."

He shook his head. "I'm happy as the handyman."

Sky's face lit up. "I heard something about a festival

coming up! I bet you could rent a table."

"No, no, no. No."

"So, that's a maybe?" The corners of her mouth twitched.

"I'm serious. They're private."

Her mouth gaped and she put the pad on the coffee table. "I'm sorry. I knocked them over. I wasn't snooping—I swear."

Jace sat and rested his hand on her knee. "I don't mind you seeing them. It's the rest of the world that I'm not so sure about."

She put her hand on top of his and squeezed. "I understand. But really, you should consider giving the world a chance."

He sighed. "Maybe."

"Really?"

"We'll see. But now, let's just keep it between you and me."

"Of course. Well, we should get back to my cottage. Haley's probably going stir crazy."

Back in the dark blue cottage, Haley sat on the couch, eating popcorn and laughing at the TV. She paused the show and turned to them. "How are you guys?"

Sky threw her arms around Jace. "Perfect."

"Oh, good!" Haley got up and put her arms around them both. "I'm so glad I could come down here and work my magic. It was my plan all along."

Sky laughed. "Sure it was." Her expression lit up. "Hey, I have an idea!"

Haley turned to Jace. "I'm not sure I like where this is going."

"I'm curious."

"That look in Sky's eyes means she's cooking up something—and in middle school, that usually meant I was probably going to wind up in trouble."

"Really?" Jace studied Sky. "I never took you for the trouble-making type."

"You two can share stories later." Sky went over to the pile of luggage, unzipped a flowered suitcase, and pulled out a camera.

"Okay, now I'm getting nervous." Jace chuckled.

Sky twisted a lens onto the front. "Since I have you both here, I want to introduce you guys to my followers. They always ask for more personal posts. What's more personal than two of my favorite people?"

Jace's stomach dropped to the floor. He had never been comfortable in front of a camera. But for Sky, he would do it.

Sky grabbed a small tripod and adjusted the camera on it on the coffee table. She faced it toward Haley who sat on the couch. She motioned for Jace to sit. He did, leaving plenty of room for Sky to sit in the middle.

"How's this going to go?" Jace asked.

"Just follow my lead, and be yourself. They'll love you!" She pressed a button on the top and a red light flashed. She plunked down in between them. "It's recording, but don't worry about messing up—I do, all the time. Anything can be edited out."

Jace and Haley exchanged a worried glance. He relaxed a little, sensing that Haley was just as nervous about being in front of Sky's audience.

"Hey, everyone!" Sky said. "Sorry this post is going up late, but it's totally worth it! You guys always ask me for more personal videos—you want to know more about the off-camera Sky. Today, I have with me one of my best friends and my boyfriend!"

Jace loved the way the word boyfriend rolled off Sky's tongue, and he couldn't be happier the title belonged to him.

Sky continued talking to the camera. "This is Haley, who I've known literally forever. We used to chase boys at recess in kindergarten. We made a few cry, didn't we?"

Haley laughed. "I think *you* did."

"What can I say?" Sky shrugged. "They used to pull our hair, and we got them to stop. Anyway, Haley has huge news—she's engaged!" Sky squealed and grabbed Haley's hand. "Speaking of huge! Take a look at this rock." She brought the ring closer to the camera. Jace assumed it would auto-focus.

They talked about the ring for a minute before Sky turned to Jace. She kissed his cheek and looked back at the camera. "And this is Jace—the best thing in Indigo

Bay! I may have come here for a variety of reasons, but he's definitely why I'm staying."

He beamed, unable to keep the grin from his face.

THIRTY-ONE

Sky pulled into the parking lot at Figaro's and found a spot near the front entrance. She turned to him with a wide grin. "I'm so glad I can make this date up to you. I feel so bad about the way the last one went. I'm sorry I was being so sensitive before."

He leaned over and gave her a quick kiss. "It's forgotten. Let's go."

They got out of the car and Sky remote-locked it. Jace walked around to her side and took her hand in his. She stared into his eyes, feeling like the luckiest person on earth. They walked into the restaurant hand-in-hand. Sky couldn't feel the ground beneath her feet. She slid on her sunglasses before they reached the doors.

"Are you always going to wear those?" Jace asked.

She flashed back to the bus full of cheerleaders. "It's either this or large, floppy hats."

"Ladies do wear those around here."

"I've noticed, and I bought one the other day."

"You did?" Jace opened the door for her. Inside, the

waiting area was so full of patrons there was standing room only.

Sky nodded. "A cute one with a light floral pattern."

"I'm sure you're beautiful wearing it."

"Welcome to Figaro's." The greeter smiled at them. "What name is the reservation under?"

"Jace Fisher."

"It'll be about fifteen minutes."

"Jace Fisher?" came a familiar feminine voice with an especially thick southern accent.

Sky turned and recognized the lady with the white dog from the pet store—the same person who had said Jace had a date with her niece.

"Miss Lucille." He smiled, but it looked forced.

Lucille said something to the dark-haired girl next to her, rose, and came over to them. "How are you, Jace?"

"Good, ma'am. I'd like you to meet Sky Hampton. She's my girlfriend."

"Girlfriend?" She turned to Sky. "You look familiar, dear. Take off your sunglasses."

Her stomach twisted in a knot, but she obliged.

The older lady nodded. "Yes, you were at Happy Paws the other day. I didn't get a chance to introduce myself."

"Nice to meet you." Sky held out her hand.

Lucille shook her hand firmly, almost hurting it. "It's my pleasure. You have a Yorkshire terrier, don't you?"

"Pixie."

"Very nice." She looked back and forth between Jace and Sky, her gaze landing on Jace. "Why don't you two take our table? It's the seat with the best view in the whole restaurant."

"We couldn't," Sky said.

Lucille turned to her. "I gave Jace a bit of a hard time before. Let me do this to make it up to him."

Sky's mouth gaped, and she turned to Jace.

"You don't have to, Miss Lucille."

"I know, but I want to. Maggie and I can sit there anytime. Figaro's belongs to my cousin's son." She took both of their hands, squeezed, and then walked over to the server, glancing back at Jace and Sky.

Sky turned to Jace. "What just happened?"

"I think we just got the best view in the place."

The server waved them over. "We're ready for you. Follow me."

Lucille smiled at them. "Have a nice dinner."

"Thank you, Miss Lucille." Jace smiled at her.

They followed the greeter through the restaurant, stopping at a table in front of an enormous picture window overlooking the bay. Sky's breath hitched. It felt like they were right on top of the water.

Jace pulled out a seat for her and scooted her in before sitting across from her.

"Your server will be Damon. He should be here shortly." He took off before either of them could thank him.

"The view is breathtaking," Jace said.

Sky turned back to the window. "It sure is."

Jace took her hand. "I meant you."

She turned back to him, her face heating. "You know, I could say the same thing about you."

"About me? I did cut my hair." He held her gaze.

"You're gorgeous—haircut or not. As wonderful as the view is, you're more breathtaking."

Someone cleared his throat next to them. "It looks like you two need some more time to look over the menus."

Jace turned to the server. "I think so."

The dark-haired man set a basket of bread in the middle of the table. "I'm Damon, your server for the evening. Would you like to start with some appetizers? Some of our house wine, perhaps?"

"What would you like?" Jace asked her.

"I'd like to try the house wine."

"Consider it done." Damon grinned and spun around, rushing off.

They looked over the menus and then into each other's eyes until Damon returned, pouring each of them a glass of dark red wine. He winked. "You'll never want another wine after this. Are you ready to order?"

"Ladies first." Jace smiled at her.

After they ordered, the server took off again.

Jace gazed into Sky's eyes and smiled. "I really

couldn't be any happier."

"Me, neither. This is perfect—you're perfect. We could be dining in a shack with no view, and I'd be just as excited."

He beamed. "I feel the same way."

They sipped the wine and made small talk until the food came. It was truly a heavenly date, as it felt like they were floating over the water. Sky had come to Indigo Bay looking for solitude, but instead managed to find true love—someone who thought she was far more interesting than her sister.

As they were finishing up, Jace took Sky's hand and looked her in the eyes. "Can I ask you something?"

"I think you just did."

He smiled. "What did I do to irritate you the last time we were here? That didn't have anything to do with Alisha, did it?"

Sky's cheeks warmed and she looked down.

"What is it?" Jace squeezed her hand.

She shook her head. "It's embarrassing."

"I want to know so I don't do it again."

"You didn't do anything wrong." She sighed, the heat creeping from her cheeks back to her neck.

"Why were you irritated, then?"

"My sister."

He gave her a double-take. "You're going to have to explain that a bit more. I don't follow."

"This is going to sound really petty."

"I promise not to think any less of you."

She may as well just spit it out. "I was jealous because you were saying how great she is."

His brows came together. "Jealous of what?"

Sky filled him in on the complicated relationship with her twin. "So, when you were saying how wonderful Aspen is, I thought I might be losing you to her, too."

Jace's mouth gaped. "What? You really thought that? How you could ever think I'd prefer the big-time, purple-haired actress to the sweet, down-to-earth sister I fell in love with?"

She stared at him.

"Sure, Aspen's great on screen but she doesn't hold a candle to you." He squeezed her hand again, and they stared into each other's eyes.

Sky was pretty sure she's somehow managed to find the perfect man.

After the meal, Jace turned to her. "I don't suppose you want to walk along that path this time?"

"Nothing would make me happier."

He led her around the building and down to a packed-dirt path. Jace slid his hand around hers and they walked in silence just feet away from the water. Hard waves crashed against the land due to the boats coming and going. Seagulls flew overhead and duck families wandered around nearby.

They came to a field of colorful wildflowers. The

sun was starting to set behind them, coloring the sky with splashes of oranges, purples, and pinks.

"Mind if we stop?" Jace asked.

Sky shook her head. "It's so beautiful, I could stay here all night."

He looked around and took a deep breath.

"Are you okay?"

Jace lowered himself to one knee and reached into his pants' pocket.

Sky's heart thundered in her chest.

He took her hand in his. "I know this may seem sudden, but though we've only known each other a short time, I feel like you've always been in my life. I certainly can't imagine living without you. You've made a world of difference to me—bringing hope and love back into my heart, and helping it to heal from all the previous losses. Will you marry me?"

Tears misted her eyes. "Yes! I'd love nothing more! I know you're the right one, so why wait?"

Relief washed over his face, followed by a wide grin. He slid the ring on her finger. It was a perfect fit. "Haley helped me figure out your ring size before she left."

Sky knelt on the ground and kissed him, tears escaping onto her cheeks.

THIRTY-TWO

Epilogue

The sun shone high in the sky over the beach. Part of it had been sectioned off for the small, private wedding. The thirty-six chairs were all filled. Sky's two brothers and their mom sat on the right. Claire sat in between Lucille and Maggie in the front row on the left. She thought Jace and Sky were Bill and Molly, but that was okay. It meant she was lucid that day, and able to attend.

Jace already stood at the altar in front of the minister. It would just be the three of them up there for the ceremony.

Sky's dad turned to her from under the shade of the trees where they stood. "Are you ready, honey?"

"I am. Just don't make me cry."

"Not before the wedding, anyway." He kissed her forehead. "I just can't believe my little girl is getting married."

"Dad…"

He winked. "Just teasing. Sort of. Looks like Aspen is about ready."

Aspen, now with dark blue hair in a long French braid and wearing a flowing, baby-blue dress, stood in front of the mic. She glanced over at Sky and Dad. He gave her a thumbs-up. Aspen nodded to the DJ.

A moment later, the music played. The tune sounded vaguely familiar, but Sky couldn't place it. Aspen had insisted on the song being a surprise. She belted out the first line, her beautiful voice dancing around the beach.

"Wait," Sky whispered. "Is that…?"

Dad hugged her. "The song you and Aspen wrote in grade school for your pretend weddings."

Sky's mouth dropped. "I can't believe she remembered." Sky had completely forgotten.

"She may be busy, but you're still part of her heart, honey."

"Dang it." Sky blinked back tears. She hadn't expected her sister to be the one who would make her cry first.

"Come on." Dad looped his arm around hers. "It's your time to shine."

As they approached, the guests all rose, but Sky's attention was focused on Jace. He was especially handsome standing there in the tuxedo. She pulled her gaze away and smiled at the guests—Haley and her fiancé, some of her other friends and family who had made it out, and some of the locals that had known Jace his whole life.

She and her father stopped at the front row and waited for the song to end. Aspen stepped back and met Sky's gaze. She smiled excitedly.

The minister stepped forward. "Who gives this bride away in marriage?"

Dad cleared his throat. "Her mother and I do." He kissed her cheek, and then sat next to Mom, who dabbed her eyes with a tissue.

A lump formed in her throat, but she turned to Jace and her heart soared. She walked over to him and he took both of her hands into his. The minister spoke about love and commitment, but she could barely focus. She was about to become Jace's wife—the luckiest woman in the world.

Finally, it was time to exchange the vows. The minister handed them both the rings. She and Jace repeated the traditional vows and slid the rings on each other's fingers.

"You may now kiss the bride."

Jace cupped her face and pressed his sweet lips on hers, deepening the kiss for a moment before pulling away with a love-struck expression that Sky was sure matched her own.

The minister stepped forward. "I'm pleased to be the first to introduce you to Mr. and Mrs. Jace and Sky Fisher."

The audience broke out into applause and Aspen sang out Sky's favorite love song from their teen years. Jace led her down the aisle, and at the end, he stopped. "You've just made me the happiest man alive."

"And you—"

He kissed her deeply again, wrapped his arms around her, lifted her up, and spun her in a circle, but her heart soared higher. Maybe he was the happiest man alive, but she was the happiest person. She'd married the man of her dreams—the sweetest of dreams.

Indigo Bay
Sweet Romance Series
Six fun beach reads by Six fabulous authors

Sweet Dreams
by Stacy Claflin

Ever since her twin became a singing sensation, Sky Hampton has struggled to be appreciated for who she is—apart from her sister. She wards off Aspen's fans, who beg for autographs and selfies everywhere Sky goes. She can't even find a guy who likes her for her. Sky flees to the small coastal town of Indigo Bay in hopes of blending in and building her blossoming career.

Jace Fisher is the textbook definition of the strong silent type—nobody can break through his tough exterior. He has suffered more than his fair share of tragedies, and to protect his shattered heart, he pushes everyone away. Jace spends his days fixing the Indigo Bay cottages, and his nights… nobody really knows. He keeps to himself.

When Jace shows up to fix Sky's AC, he barely notices her and she's distracted with settling in. It takes an emergency situation to get them talking, and when they do, the two find they have more in common than first appeared. As their attraction grows, defenses soar. Will they be able to risk love when they've both been burned in the past?

Sweet Matchmaker

by Jean Oram

Ginger McGinty hates liars. And she just married a spy.

Bridal shop owner Ginger McGinty excels at matchmaking unless it's for herself. That is, until she meets the dreamy Aussie who helps her get into an event meant for engaged couples. Logan Stone is sweet, caring, thoughtful and fun—everything she desires in a man. But it turns out, her new fake fiancé could use a bit more than just a pretend engagement to get him into parties—he needs a quick marriage keep him in the country so he can be with his adopted special needs daughter.

With a marriage of convenience pro-con list longer than the average wedding veil, Ginger puts her faith in romance and offers Logan her hand in return for one thing—no lies.

But little does she know, almost everything she knows about her new husband is based on a lie.

Everything except his kisses and the way he accidentally spills his soul whenever they meet. And that's quickly becoming a problem for Logan Stone who depends on distance and deceit to keep civilians such as Ginger safe from his enemy's clutches.

Will the two find love in their marriage of convenience, or will everything break apart when the truth rises to the surface, shattering everything, including their trust?

Sweet Sunrise

by Kay Correll

Sometimes life has a way of teaching lessons whether you're ready to learn them or not...

The last place on earth Will Layton wants to be is Indigo Bay, but his younger sister needs him and he's never been able to say no to her. But she left out a few details... like their father staying with her and the girl who dumped him years ago is living right next door.

The last person Dr. Ashley Harden thought she'd see in Indigo Bay is Will Layton, but he's back in town and just as irresistible as when they were young. Seeing Will again is a complication that isn't on her carefully mapped out life plan.

In spite of Ashley's best intentions, she starts falling for Will again, but nothing has changed. She's still focused on getting the townspeople to accept her and see her as more than the girl from the wrong side of town, while Will is determined to guard his heart at any cost.

Not the easiest road to true love... especially when secrets from the past are revealed and history threatens to repeat itself.

Sweet Illusions

by Jeanette Lewis

Eva Malone was very young when her mother forced the family to join a violent doomsday cult, but she remembers a little about how normal life used to be. As a young woman, she escapes the cult and relocates to Indigo Bay, South Carolina to pursue her dream of peaceful anonymity.

After several tumultuous years as a policeman in Atlanta, Ben Andrews has had enough. He returns home to Indigo Bay and joins the Indigo Bay PD, where the most exciting part of the job is getting a kitten out of a tree or rescuing tourists who lose their keys at the beach.

Eva and Ben are immediately drawn to each other. But as the prophesied date of the apocalypse draws near and the cult steps up its efforts to find her, Eva realizes she can't maintain her sweet illusion forever.

Sweet Regrets

by Jennifer Peel

Melanie Dixon never thought she would find herself divorced, pregnant, and living back with her parents in Indigo Bay. Not one to let misfortune get the best of her, she picks up the broken pieces of her life and bit by bit puts them back together. She's determined to go it alone, but her loving and equally determined family and friends have another idea.

Enter Declan Shaw, the boy next door from long ago. The boy she wasn't quite ready to commit forever to at eighteen. Back in Indigo Bay due to a recent job promotion, Declan sees this as a second chance to reunite with the girl who has owned his heart since the day they met in their junior year of high school. But Melanie is a tougher sell on the idea than he thought she would be. Now it's up to him to prove to Melanie that she can trust him with her heart and that he's the man she and her baby deserve.

Will the regret and hurt of the past win out? Or will love prevail?

Sweet Rendezvous
by Danielle Stewart

On her last tank of gas Elaine Mathews drives South. Spontaneity had never been her strength, but there was something about being publicly fired that had a way of changing things. An empty bank account, broken heart, and enough humiliation to last a life time was all Elaine could claim as her own. Her car choked to a stop in the quiet beach town of Indigo Bay and all she could do was sit on the curb and wait for the sun to set on her misery.

Davis Mills has a routine. Wake. Work. Eat. Sleep. Repeat. It hadn't always been that way. He'd left indigo bay once and returned a broken man. Now he kept his dreams small and his schedule tight. If there was no room in his life for anything new then he'd never repeat his mistakes.

When fate has them, quite literally colliding Elaine and Davis are faced with an important question. Can you live a full life if you never take a risk? Or is life made up of every mistake, miracle and chance that comes with being in love?

For purchase links and other information:

stacyclaflin.com/books/indigo-bay-sweet-romance-series

If you enjoyed *Sweet Dreams*, you'll love the Hunters! You may want to start with Bayside Promises, which is Haley's story of finding love despite a painful past. (Read a sneak peek after the list of books.) Or you can start at the beginning with the Seaside Hunters! It's up to you...

The Hunters

Meet the Hunter brothers of Kittle Falls...

The Seaside Hunters novels are a series of contemporary sweet romances. They're set in the charming beach town of Kittle Falls, following the California Hunters as they make their way back to their hometown and find the loves they couldn't elsewhere.

The Seaside Hunters

stacyclaflin.com/books/seaside-series

Seaside Surprises

Work hard. Play often. Love unconditionally.

Tiffany Saunders is on the run. When she winds up stranded in a seaside town, she wants nothing more than to forget her horrific past and kept moving. But a chance meeting with a handsome local changes everything.

Jake Hunter has some deep emotional scars and is trying to cope with running the family business. The last thing he wants is a relationship—until a mysterious brunette walks into his store and complicates it all.

Tiffany prefers to keep the painful memories of the past where they belong—in her rear view mirror. But dark secrets cannot stay hidden forever. Just as the walls around Tiffany's heart start to come down, the past catches up with her. Will true love be able to conquer all?

Seaside Heartbeats

Sometimes love shows up when you least expect it.

After years of hard work, architect Lana Summers just wants a relaxing vacation in the beach town of Kittle Falls. Instead, she suffers unexpected heart problems, and finds herself in the office of a gorgeous cardiologist—who only makes her heart work harder.

Brayden Hunter left his successful cardiology practice in Dallas to be closer to his aging parents. Focused on building a health care clinic in his hometown, he doesn't want any distractions. However, the beautiful Lana is one he can't seem to avoid.

As their attraction grows, they stumble upon a 160-year-old mystery. Brayden catches her adventurous spirit as they chase after answers, and he can't help falling for her. But can he convince her to stay in the small beach town and with him?

Seaside Dances

Dream big. Dance often. Love completely.

Zachary Hunter is no stranger to rejection. After multiple failed efforts to get his novel published in New York, he's counting on a trip home to turn his luck around.

Jasmine Blackwell has big dreams. She hopes her internship as a dance instructor in Kittle Falls will be the stepping stone she needs to achieve her lifelong goals.

After a chance meeting, neither Zachary nor Jasmine can deny their attraction. They fear their aspirations are too big to let a relationship tie them down. Can they have both love and the careers of their dreams?

Seaside Kisses

People change, but some feelings last forever.

Rafael Hunter never thought he'd return to Kittle Falls, but life gave him no other choice. Los Angeles chewed him up, spit him out, and sent him back to square one.

Amara Fowler has lived in the small beach town her entire life. She's overcome her shyness to grow into the woman she always knew she could be, but she never forgot her secret crush. When the alluring Rafael returns, he can't help but stir in her a whirlwind of old feelings.

They've both changed so much. Has life kept them incompatible or has it molded them into a matching set?

Seaside Christmas

He can't stand her. She thinks he's crazy. Will their feelings stay etched in permanent ink?

Cruz Hunter has always stuck out in his small hometown. Now that he's covered in tattoos, the residents peg him as even more of an outcast. It seems like the whole world is against his dream of opening a local tattoo parlor.

When he finally finds the perfect place for his new business, Cruz discovers a pastor and his daughter have already bought it. The only thing more irritating than the change in his plan is Talia, a beautiful and feisty argument in a dress. Cruz would like nothing more than to have her out of his life and his mind, but for some reason, she's the only thing he can think about.

If Cruz and Talia can stop arguing long enough, opposites may do much more than attract.

Purchase links.
stacyclaflin.com/books/seaside-series

Meet the Hunter siblings of Enchantment Bay...

We met three of them in the Seaside series: Logan, Sullivan, and Dakota. Now we finally get to meet the "babies" of the family – twins, Freya and Shale. They're all about to meet the loves of their lives, they just don't know it yet!

If you enjoyed your time with the Seaside Hunters, you'll love spending time with their Oregon cousins!

The Bayside Hunters

stacyclaflin.com/bayside-series

Bayside Wishes

She's guarding a family secret. He's investigating a murder. Will a second homecoming lead to true love?

Freya Hunter is living the fabulous life. The west-coast girl rakes it in as a fashion model in New York City, but everything changes after she returns home for a quick visit.

The reunion with friends and family in Enchantment Bay is sweet, especially when she hits it off with Nico Valentin, a ruggedly handsome police sergeant. As Nico investigates a murder, Freya learns a family secret big enough to turn her world upside down.

Freya is torn between her new life and her hometown—the life she loves vs. the brother who needs her and the sergeant who wants her. When her decision doesn't go nearly as well as she planned, she wonders if she can help her brother and keep her growing feelings for Nico at bay before they consume her.

Bayside Evenings

She's single and stuck. His relationship is going nowhere. Will the next wedding they plan… be their own?

Dakota Hunter is great at wedding planning but terrible at finding a guy. Each one she encounters is worse than the one before… until she meets Clay. There's one teensy problem: her attractive new assistant has a long-term girlfriend.

Clay Harper is thrilled to land his new job with Dakota, surrounding himself with happy couples day in and day out. But when he sees true love in person, he realizes his own relationship is far less than happy. It doesn't help that being around Dakota feels easy. It feels right.

As Dakota and Clay grow a deeper connection, Clay's girlfriend refuses to go down without a fight. Can the wedding planners go from seeing happy couples… to being one?

Bayside Promises

She's wounded. He's driven. Could they be exactly what the other needs?

Ten years earlier, Haley Faraway fled home without looking back. After her father's death, she reluctantly returns to Enchantment Bay to help her mom and sister. Painful memories haunt her, and Haley finds herself pouring her heart out to the one person she least expected—the impossibly gorgeous, albeit short-tempered, Sullivan Hunter.

Sullivan wants nothing more than to focus on his newly-acquired realty business. But when Haley comes back to town, he can't deny his attraction to her. After a string of bad relationships with gold-digging women, she's a breath of fresh air. Or is she? Just as he begins to get comfortable with their burgeoning relationship, he discovers she's a realtor, too. His temper gets the best of him as he suspects he's being used by yet another woman.

Every time Haley and Sullivan clear one hurdle, another looms larger in their path and they push each other away. Can they move on from from their painful pasts and find love—or are they doomed to repeat old mistakes?

Bayside Destinies and **Bayside Promises** are coming soon!

Purchase Links: Bayside Hunters.
stacyclaflin.com/bayside-series

Sign up for new release updates. (And get some free novels, too.)
stacyclaflin.com/newsletter

Seaside Hunters Short Stories

Seaside Beginnings

This is the story of Robert and Dawn, the five Hunter brothers' parents. We meet them in each of the Seaside books, and they've grown on readers almost as much as the brothers themselves. Now we get a glimpse into their story.

Seaside Memories

Sophia is the youngest of the Hunter siblings. Each of her brothers hold her memory in a special place. Her story is one of first love, second chances, and enjoying life.

Seaside Treasures

Allen and Jackie's story is of an unlikely love and healing old wounds. They couldn't be more different, but that could be exactly what they need.

Read these and many other short stories in Tiny Bites, a snack-sized multi-genre collection by Stacy Claflin.

stacyclaflin.com/books/short-stories

Preview of *Bayside Promises*

Haley Faraway took a deep breath as she stepped into the large, elegant wedding hall. Why had she let her sister talk her into this?

She pulled some loose blonde hair behind her ear, straightened her back, and followed the noise of conversation. It led her down a sweet-smelling hallway decorated with beautiful summer flowers. She came to a set of already-open double doors leading outside.

"Are you here for the bride or groom?" asked an usher in a tuxedo.

Neither. Haley cleared her throat. She had sort of known the bride a long time ago. "The bride."

Her heart raced, threatening to break through her ribcage and ruin her new turquoise dress.

The usher held out his elbow. "Come with me."

Haley linked her arm through his and hoped he didn't notice her shaking.

He stopped walking next to the seats on the left side. "Do you see anyone you would like to sit with, ma'am?"

Ma'am? What was she, sixty?

"No, I'm by myself."

The usher walked her a few rows down and gestured for her to take a seat. Haley thanked him and sat on the far end, giving actual friends and family a chance to sit by the aisle the bride would walk down soon enough. Haley adjusted the fabric of her dress, pulled out her phone, and pretended to be busy with it.

Someone squeezed Haley's bare shoulder. She glanced up to see the high schooler sporting blue streaks in her dark hair, a nose ring, and an eyebrow piercing. "Thanks for coming." The tough-looking girl smiled with confidence, but Haley could see straight through her baby sister's bravado to the insecurity underneath.

Haley forced a smile. "You'll do great, Jensyn."

She nodded. "I really need this job."

"Yeah, you do, but don't think about that. Just focus on what needs to be done. You've always been a hard worker. Just tap into that."

Jensyn twirled a strand of blue around her finger. "That was a long time ago, Hales. You haven't been back to Enchantment Bay since I was seven."

Haley squirmed in the seat. She wouldn't have been back if Mom hadn't begged and pleaded with her to keep an eye on Jensyn over the summer. Haley squeezed Jensyn's arm. "And now we finally get to know each other beyond screen time."

Jensyn's gaze darted to the back of the courtyard. "I gotta go. Wish me luck. This is my boss's wedding. No pressure."

"You're a Faraway. You'll do great."

"I hope so." Jensyn ran back.

Haley jumped when her phone beeped with a text. She muted the device and checked the message. It was from Mom.

How are my girls?

Good. Jensyn talked me into coming to the wedding.

She didn't wear that short leather skirt, did she?

No. Black pants.

Oh, good. I can't thank you enough for watching her this summer. Aunt Elma's place is worse than I thought.

Don't worry about us. Just get her house ready to sell.

You'll help with that?

Yes, Mom. The wedding's going to start soon. Talk later.

Thanks again.

Haley stuffed her phone inside her purse and glanced around for any familiar faces. After ten years away from the small town she'd grown up in, everyone and everything had changed. She had done her best to put everything about Enchantment Bay out of her mind during those years. In all that time, she hadn't kept in touch with anyone, choosing instead to focus on her work as a realtor and spending most of her waking hours working her way up in the company.

Three chatty couples filed down her row. Haley brought out her phone again, hoping they wouldn't pay her any attention.

"Oh, my gosh. Haley? Haley Faraway?"

So much for that. She slid her phone back into her purse and glanced over to see Elena Todd.

Her big blue eyes widened. "You look amazing, girl! I never thought I'd see you again. Not after the way you took off right after graduation."

Haley forced a smile. "I've been busy."

"I heard." Elena wrapped her arms around Haley. "Is it true you're a big shot real estate agent?"

She hugged Elena back with stiff arms. "I wouldn't say big shot, but I'm doing pretty well for myself."

Elena released her hold. "I'm really sorry about your dad. He was so young."

Haley nodded. She probably needed to come up with a pat answer to that, as everyone would likely bring up his untimely death. But what was an appropriate reply when a parent was shot and killed in a bar fight? She needed a canned response for the people who asked why she didn't come to his funeral, too. Not that any of it was anyone's business. "Well, it—"

"I'm so excited about Dakota's wedding, aren't you?" Elena's eyes shone. "She's planned so many weddings—even celebrity weddings, did you know that?—I'll bet hers is to die for." She turned and gushed over the decorations.

"I'll bet it is." Haley glanced around the stunning courtyard. Soft music played from a couple harpists. Flowers of every color and shape hung everywhere she could see.

Dakota Hunter was the little sister of Sullivan, best friend of Haley's high school sweetheart, Jackson. Dakota and Haley had known each other through Sullivan, so at least Haley wasn't crashing a complete stranger's wedding just to give Jensyn moral support on her first day of work.

The music grew louder, and the conversations all hushed. A bridesmaid and groomsman walked down the aisle, arm in arm. Though it took a moment, Haley recognized the bridesmaid. It was Freya Hunter, Dakota and Sullivan's youngest sister. She had long, thick dark hair and an enormous smile—every bit as gorgeous as every other Hunter sibling.

The next couple was a girl she barely recognized from high school and Sullivan Hunter. Haley's breath caught. He'd grown even more handsome over the last decade, and he'd really filled out. Wow, had he filled out. He'd been good-looking back then, but now... It was as though he'd stepped off a runway.

She stared at him as he made his way down the aisle. Who had been lucky enough to marry him? There was no way he was still single. Haley couldn't take her gaze away from him as the rest of the wedding party made their way onto the platform.

Finally, everyone rose. She cleared her throat and tried to forget about Sullivan. He certainly wasn't a distraction she needed. Keeping Jensyn out of trouble would be a full-time job outside of the difficulties of trying to sell houses in a town she wasn't familiar with anymore.

Dakota came down the aisle with her dad. Tears shone in his eyes despite the grin on his face. It was nice to know some fathers actually cared about their daughters. Dakota still had the same stunning red hair she'd had as a kid. It was beautifully braided into a crown with small white flowers woven into it. The gown sparkled in the sunlight and flowed behind her as she walked. She was a vision, but her gaze focused solely on her soon-to-be husband.

Her dad gave her away and then took a seat in the front row next to his wife and the two other Hunter siblings who weren't in the wedding—Shale, Freya's twin, and Logan, the oldest of the bunch.

Haley tried to focus on the ceremony but found her attention kept landing on Sullivan. She'd never thought of him in a romantic way back in high school because she'd only had eyes for Jackson back then. Now she couldn't help wondering how things might be different if she'd have chosen Sullivan instead of Jackson.

Not that any of it mattered. She would have fled town right after graduation to get away from her father's drunken rages and verbal abuse. Tears stung her eyes. It was bad enough that she had to spend the summer in that house full of painful memories. Would everything in town remind her of what she'd run from? She wiped her eyes and sniffled.

Elena put her hand on Haley's arm. "I know. It's such a beautiful ceremony."

Purchase links:

stacyclaflin.com/bayside-series

OTHER BOOKS BY STACY CLAFLIN

If you enjoy reading outside the romance genre, you may enjoy some of Stacy Claflin's other books, also. She's a *USA Today* bestselling author who writes about complex characters overcoming incredible odds. Whether it's her Gone saga of psychological thrillers, her various paranormal romance tales, or her sweet romance series, Stacy's three-dimensional characters shine through bringing an experience readers don't soon forget.

The Hunters

Seaside Surprises

Seaside Heartbeats

Seaside Dances

Seaside Kisses

Seaside Christmas

Bayside Wishes

Bayside Evenings

Bayside Promises

Bayside Destinies

Bayside Dreams

The Gone Saga
The Gone Trilogy: Gone, Held, Over

Dean's List

No Return

Alex Mercer Thrillers
Girl in Trouble

Turn Back Time

Curse of the Moon
Lost Wolf

Chosen Wolf

Hunted Wolf

Broken Wolf

Cursed Wolf

The Transformed Series

Main Series

Deception

Betrayal

Forgotten

Ascension

Duplicity

Sacrifice

Destroyed

Transcend

Entangled

Dauntless

Obscured

Partition

Visit StacyClaflin.com for details.

Sign up for new release updates and receive three free ebooks.
stacyclaflin.com/newsletter

Want to hang out and talk about books? Join My Book Hangout and participate in the discussions. There are also exclusive giveaways, sneak peeks and more. Sometimes the members offer opinions on book covers, too. You never know what you'll find.
facebook.com/groups/stacyclaflinbooks

Made in United States
North Haven, CT
26 May 2022

19523993R00136